Uncommon Pie & Other Stories
Ajesh Sharma

My thanks go out to a couple of special people.

Rita, my dear wife and best friend, it was you who never quit telling me I should write a collection of short stories. Well, here they are!

Ganesh, thank you for your help! It was invaluable!

This book is a work of fiction. The names, characters and incidents portrayed in it are the work of the author's imagination. Any resemblance to actual persons, living or dead, business establishments, events or locales is entirely coincidental.

Without limiting the rights under copyright reserved above, no part of this publication may be reproduced, stored in a retrieval system, or transmitted, in any form or by any means (electronic, mechanical, photocopying, recording or otherwise), without the express prior written permissions of the publisher. The scanning, uploading, and distribution of this book via the internet or via any other means without the permission of the publisher is illegal and punishable by law.

This book is sold subject to the conditions that it shall not, by way of trade or otherwise, be lent, re-sold, hired out or otherwise circulated without the publisher's prior consent in any form of binding or cover other than that in which it is published and without a similar condition including this condition being imposed on the subsequent purchaser.

SloWord Books, Mississauga, Canada
ISBN 978-0-9959271-3-1
International edition
Copyright © 2024 Ajesh Sharma
All rights reserved
Cover photography by Ajesh Sharma

Foreword

The writer's life has often been romanticised, with images of a struggling artist, writing by the light of the guttering candle in the attic, or the lonely hut in the woods, depicting the talented writer working away under crippling conditions in order to be true to his art.

The reality, in my situation, is quite different.

I'm sitting here in a welllit basement, with an electric desk that hosts two large monitors, a freshly brewed cup of coffee, a modern computer with software that checks basic grammar and typographical errors in real time. I've paid my bills by spending forty years working in the technology industry, so food and drink are not in short supply.

It would seem, thus, that there is no resistance to the actual work of writing, in my case.

In actual fact, this writer's life has not been without challenges, for the real hindrance to the writing of a story is in the head. How does one take an idea, build it, develop it to a logical conclusion and then write it down into a coherent flow of words that compel the reader to follow the story to the end?

The desk, the lights, the coffee, the snacks, the software are distractions in themselves. The real issue is the chaotic flow of thoughts in the writer's head. Most of the time for me, the ideas refuse to become plots. This is, probably, due to the undisciplined nature of my brain, which is easily distracted by social media, the guitar that sits behind me to the right, the technological challenges of maintaining the website, going for long walks with the beloved, time spent cooing and making faces at grandkids, the cooking, eating and other exigencies of life.

In short, I'm, well, never mind all that now, you want to read what I have to say about the stories in this book, right?

Well, this can be truly said to have started with a story that appeared on my website in 2013. It was the first piece of pure fiction I had ever written.

This was called "The Angler on the Credit" and it came from a chance encounter with a taxi driver on a cool autumn evening in Canada. Everything, but the situation at the end, is fictional. I have modified that early version of this story and included it here.

Two years later, in 2015, I wrote another short story. This one gained a life of its own and eventually grew into "A Couple of Choices". It was released as a 3 act play in Kindle format in December 2017.

Also, in 2017, two of my short stories were published in two different magazines.

Man with a Plan appeared in Telegram Magazine in March 2017, and Carpe Diem first appeared in Unbound Magazine in June 2017. Both of these had different titles, but they have been modified and developed, and they have, therefore, been given new titles to better capture the essence of the story.

The year 2017 can, thus, be deemed my most prolific year for putting stuff out there for you to read.

Since then, I've been asked by some people, when I was going to release anything new. This is a question I have asked myself every hour on the hour.

And now, the hour, or day, or month, or year is here!

2024 is the year, in which the second edition of "A Couple of Choices" was released in both print and ebook formats. The print edition was long overdue, due to laziness, work, and a general air of helplessness, and travel! Mustn't forget travel.

With this out of the way, I heaved a deep sigh of relief, and got to work on the other manuscripts I had lying around on hard drives. Much pruning, many sticky notes, deep sighs and eyerolls later, I decided on this collection of twenty one short stories.

A few of these stories started as responses to writing prompts from various sources. In many cases, the prompts expected flash fiction, with a word limit of around 100 to 300.

Some of these appeared on my website. I treated them as snippets, synopses, something to be used at a future point in time to build a fully developed story, with characters that showed some depth, and the action had some background.

I spent a fair bit of time looking at these pieces, piecing them together, combining them, building characters, and developing the backdrop. The goal was to add texture, widen and deepen the characters and their story. So you know now that these stories are rather longer than 200 words!

If you've read some of those little pieces, as they appeared on my website or on social media, you might recognize elements of them in some of the stories here.

Now the big question, what sort of stories are these. What should you expect? Where are they set?

Well, the stories in this collection are of various types. The stories are set in different areas of the world, with characters and conditions that may have been borrowed from my own recollections on my journeys. What you can expect is an exploration of life in various ways.

There's a tiny bit of fantasy, but isn't all fiction fantasy?

There's a bit of light romance, but isn't romance what we all need?

There are a couple of thrillers, but isn't that why we read, to be carried away and thrilled?

There's some humour in there, but isn't humour essential to one's being?

The stories are about birth, life, love, death, thrills and chills and relationships, real or perceived, and human behaviour.

To answer your next question, yes, there may be a death or two.

I do hope you enjoy these stories.

Thank you for investing your precious time and hard earned wealth into my work.

Ajesh Sharma © 2024

Late

As the world around him moved faster and faster, he found himself later and later.

'twas ever thus, as Shakespeare would have said.

It wasn't that he didn't try. He did.

He woke up earlier, ate faster, and dressed quicker. When he arrived at work, though, he found he was late. Everyone, it seemed, had been hard at work for hours before he showed up. In the early days, he'd mutter brief apologies, which were usually ignored. He then turned to making facetious comments as he walked in. Nobody seemed to understand what he said.

In any case, they were busy, very busy. They always had very important presentations to prepare, or very important meetings to attend or very important action items to take care of after the very important presentation had been presented to very important people at the very important meeting.

He was always a few minutes early for each meeting. Everyone else came in a few minutes beyond the start time.

He sometimes thought this was poor form and indicated to other people that he was unimportant. Important people seemed to be busy and were late to meetings.

The meetings, thus, never started on time and never accomplished anything because, usually, people had to rush off to some other, more important, meeting. To which they arrived late as well.

The other time he wasn't late was for social events. There were occasions when he was the first person to arrive. Everyone else straggled in thirty or more minutes later. They never apologized for their lateness, and their lack of punctuality was ignored.

It was only his seemingly late arrival for work that seemed to mark him out as a slacker.

At the meeting, or at the social event, he was quickly relegated to the background as the go getters at work and the social butterflies went on to impress, enthrall and entice the audience. At work, they were promoted or were given responsibilities that recognised their contribution to the cause.

He never really understood how they managed to be early for work and late for everything they did at work and yet receive accolades. He could not fathom how everyone was always busy, but there were never any outcomes that looked desirable to someone who saw and observed. He read the official announcement of success and marveled at their ability to craft a message of great success, even though the previously stated outcomes had not been realized.

Forty years he worked, and for forty years, he remained clueless, confused and confounded by the confidence of everyone around him.

He was not late for retirement.

He chose his time and retired; some would have said early to do so. He didn't mind. He had things he felt he had to think about, things he felt he wanted to do and he didn't need any more of the constant supply of disapproval and disappointment in the way he did things.

He went for his daily walks. He sat on the bench, just off the walkway in the park a couple of kilometres from his house. He watched the walkers, joggers and children pass him by. The baseball game in summer kept him engaged for a few minutes before he headed home.

He didn't think he was lonely. He didn't miss any of his colleagues. He hadn't gone to any of their funerals.

His life was quiet, spent in walks, with Padma, the stories he tried to write and the general air of waiting for something to happen.

When it did, he found himself on the floor of the bedroom. It was late in the day and the night was spent in hospital, connected to tubes and needles.

The diagnosis came the next afternoon. It was definite. Sobs and cries of grief and concern accompanied it

His only son Rahul, got off the cellphone long enough to hear it. His daughter-in-law, Sunita, stopped trying to cajole the eleven year old, Raju, into having the snack she had carried for him.

His wife, Padma, listened to the doctor carefully, asked pertinent questions.

Once the doctor had left, he started coughing, a prolonged fit.

Padma shooed everyone out of the room and shut the door. As she turned, the coughing stopped.

"Well, what is it?" she asked him.

"How did you know I wanted them out of here? Never mind. Sixty years of knowing me", he waved her to the chair.

"The doctor says two weeks or three at the most. I wondered if I should write a letter," he said.

"To whom?"

He said, "Rahul and Sunita. The way they live. Rahul is my only child and I see his life, glued to the cellphone, the sort of stuff that drives that family. I see little Raju and I ..." he tailed off at the look in her eye.

"And so you want to write a letter to show them the error of their ways and bring them to the primrose path of glorious life and all its wonders", she finished it for him.

"I wish you'd tone down that sarcasm a bit. I mean, I only have two weeks to live."

"Maybe three. Too late now, I'm 75, you're 78 and almost dead. So if I can't change, and you shouldn't even bother, why do you think your letter is going to change anyone?"

"I hate that you're right all the time!"

"Look, four months ago they said three weeks is all you had. Who can tell what how long you have left? You were always late for everything, remember?"

"True."

She stared at him and reached out for his hand.

"You know, you've lived a long life. We've had some good times together and some bad times. Everyone does. It's normal. If you haven't been able to reach anyone all these years, and make them listen to you, it's not meant to be. They won't get it. You need to let it go."

"You know, all those years, working with all these people. I couldn't get through to them. I could not understand what drove them, how they thought and why they did what they did. I tried so hard to build a connection. Just so I could understand, so I could help them."

"And there's your problem. You should have got on with your own life and let them be. There were days I would despair of you actually being with me. Seeing what you had, what we had between us. I finally realized you were an idiot who didn't know better. Then I let you be."

"I'm sorry. I was always trying to make sense of everything. I realize now you can't know everything and you have to know when to stop and let it go. And now it's too late."

They sat there in silence, hand in hand. Then it was time for her to go home.

Like every projected outcome promised by so many executives he had known over the years, the two week completion date did not happen. Nine months passed by with no end in sight.

And then, one night, Padma went to sleep and never woke up as she usually did, at 6 AM.

Once the cremation was done and all the mourners had gone to pursue their own lives, he was alone again.

More months went by as he waited. The walks were tedious without Padma. He sat in his veranda, doing crosswords. Then he was back in the hospital bed. Alone again. Doctors came and went, nurses fussed around. He was dimly aware through his semi comatose state that there was activity around him.

In his mind, the thoughts raced at bewildering speed. Most of them focused on the time when he had entered the hospital months ago. Padma, the only person who he thought he understood, and who he thought understood him, had walked beside him as he was wheeled into the room.

Padma had been gone for months now, but as he lay there, with his breathing shallow, under the mask, the various monitors showing graphs of his vital signs, he thought he heard her voice calling him.

"Come on, now, hurry up. You're late again."

AJESH SHARMA

There was a doctor in the room. He was talking to the nurse.

"Well, looks like he's almost there now. All the signs are clear. A couple of hours. You had better get the family in. Won't be long now."

He was sure that's what the doctor was saying. He wanted to speak. He wanted to clarify. He wanted to know the percentage of confidence the doctor had. He'd been pretty confident before, months ago. What would the family do around him? Could they help in any way? Wouldn't they just get in the way, wringing their hands, sobbing and sniffling?

He couldn't speak.

"I'm not late, everyone's early", were his last thoughts.

Six months later, his portrait went up next to Padma's in the alcove above the TV in Rahul's house.

Late, again.

The Train Conductor

The diesel sat at the platform in the early morning gloom. The winter day was just starting and the misty air growing lighter as the sun grew stronger. The dew coated coaches lay asleep with droplets developing at the windows and door handles.

Coach reservation charts started to appear, as the attendant walked down the train, pasting each on the side of the bogeys as he went. A small crowd followed him, checking each list. Some passengers had coolies following them with baggage on their head.

As they identified their coach, the sleepy platform came awake with the yelled directions, exhortations and urgent urgings, as the passengers pushed and heaved their luggage onboard. The coaches filled up with travelers peering at the seat numbers and their reservations. Bags were counted and recounted and children exhorted to stay close.

As the time for departure came closer, the noise levels rose as the big diesel engine rumbled deeply into life. There was a puff of smoke and then the exhaust misted the cold air in a steady plume of white condensation.

Tapas Paul dropped his bag into his little cabin at the end of the train, checked his watch and stepped off the train.

Tapas was the conductor on the Maitree Express.

AJESH SHARMA

His job was to ensure that the train covered the distance from Kolkata Station, formerly called Chitpur Station, to the Gede – Darshana Zero Point, the railway halt just inside the border of Bangladesh. Here he would hand over his duties to his Bangladeshi counterpart, who would then see the train through all the way to Dhaka, its terminal point.

When asked, Tapas always had a non-committal answer. It was a job. More importantly, it was a government job. A regular pension, security of income and regular hours were guaranteed. The job itself was physically not exhausting. It did require alertness, a certain level of meticulous planning and follow through, but it was not otherwise demanding.

He checked the big clock under the sloping rafters of the platform and compared the time with his watch. It was 0709 hours. He walked a short way down the train, his flag tucked under his arm, making sure all the coach doors were shut. Then he walked back to his conductor's coach, put one leg on the iron step. He checked his watch, found it was 0710. He pulled the flag out and waved it, while blowing his whistle. He got an answering wave from the engine.

Tapas climbed aboard and the diesel took on a deeper note. The exhaust went dark as the train jerked forward. The cold wheels screeched, straining for grip on the cold rail, easing as the train slid forward. The families who had come to see people off, waved and cried out to the passengers who leaned out shouting goodbyes, and last minute instructions were passed both ways.

As the train gathered speed and pulled out from the station, Tapas, keeping an eye out from the back, went in to his cabin. It was a cold day in Kolkata and Tapas, bundled up with a cap, a muffler around his neck and a sweater under his jacket, had no desire to stay out in the air.

The Maitree Express gathered speed and headed northeast on its way to the capital of Bangladesh. Tapas settled down to his charts and checklists, making sure all the forms were filled out. Then he started his walk down the train, checking passengers off his list as he went. He offered suggestions on baggage stowage, making sure to clear the walkways. He worked methodically, routine born of repetition.

Once all the checks and paperwork was done, he settled down to his breakfast. This consisted of a boiled egg, salted and peppered to his satisfaction, two small wheat rotis and a potato curry. He topped it off with tea.

His lunch awaited him in Gede, once he had handed over the train.

He packed up the empty tin of food, sat back and sipped his tea. His gave himself to his thoughts, which were mostly about music.

He looked forward to the Friday evening sessions with the rest of the musicians. There was Sujata, with a voice that held a note like a strand of silk held a spider. Kunal played guitar with chords that were strange, but somehow matched the cadence and keys of the song. Amol's harmonium was always there to provide the backdrop to the song.

And there was Tapas with his tabla.

Tabla, to Tapas, made life bearable, even enjoyable. He had learned to play tabla as a boy. His father's younger brother had seen the interest and taken him under his wing, teaching him the first basic rhythms. For five years, Tapas would spend an hour a day next door with his uncle. His uncle was delighted to see that Tapas understood the drums, the beats, the cadence required. Clearly, the young lad was a natural, he said.

When his uncle died, taken in the middle of the night by a coronary, Tapas inherited the set. No one objected, because no one cared to take them over and everyone could see that Tapas wanted it.

He loved the sounds he could generate from the two oddly shaped drums, the movement of hands, fingers and the angle of the elbows and the balls of the hands bringing out subtle changes in timbre that were essential flavours to each song. He played every day, after school. His mother spoke to his father about having someone tutor him and he was sent off to learn from Kantida.

Kantida, was the town eccentric, with seemingly no source of income and no family. He did have a collection of musical instruments, including a piano, and he could play them all. There were persistent rumours that he was the beneficiary of a certain lady, a Frenchwoman. Kantida spoke about his travels in Europe, three decades in the past, with a passionless manner that failed to camouflage his joy. He made no mention about any women in his past. He also spoke French and English with equal felicity.

Tapas had time on the route to think about his music. He could sit at his post and mimic the movements he would make if he had his table with him. The only thing other than the table he cared about was food.

As the train made its familiar way through the countryside that he had come to ignore, he thought about his lunch and from there he thought about Aparna. Fifteen years into his marriage, two children lost, Tapas had long since decided not to think of the tragedy. Aparna, too, had resigned herself to her life.

As the train neared the border, Tapas checked his papers, and did a walk-by through the coaches. He liked to make sure he was handing over the train with the paperwork done and checked.

The train slowed to crawl as it approached Gede before stopping short of the station. After a few minutes, it shook itself, as if awaking from deep thought and edged forward and came to a hissing stop at the platform. Tapas, leaning out at the back, didn't wait for the train to come to a complete halt. He was off the train and onto the platform, with a few quickened steps to match the speed of the train.

He walked leisurely forward to meet the Bangladeshi conductor, Moinul, who would take over the train and manage it onwards to Dhaka. Paperwork was checked, pens moved swiftly over the paper, making tick marks, underlining sections. Signatures were put on and then Tapas walked back to the conductor's cabin with Moinul.

He picked up his bag, said goodbye to Moinul with a clasp of the shoulder and stepped off the train to the conductor's waiting room. It was time for lunch and Tapas had the perfect place for a train conductor's lunch.

Two hundred and fifty metres down the road from the station was a little shack. A brazier blazed, the big wok sizzling with vegetables and curries. Tapas sat down to a fresh hot meal. Once it was done, he lay on the coir bed laid out under the shade of the tree and took a nap.

Precisely at 1pm, he walked back to the station and awaited the arrival of the Maitree Express heading back to Kolkata. The ritual of paperwork completed, this time in reverse, Tapas flagged off the train and headed back to Kolkata. Just after 4pm, the train hummed into the station at Kolkata and by 4:30pm, Tapas was done for the day.

He picked up his bicycle from the shop that stored the bicycles of the daily commuters for a monthly fee. He rode home, the twenty minutes easy and boring from years of practice. He hailed the regulars on his path, the manager of the store selling aluminium pots and pans and other kitchen artifacts, the sweet shop, the little teashop where the big pot of tea bubbled all day behind the debris of a thousand smashed earthen teacups.

He changed, washed and sat down to his tea and biscuits which arrived at the same time that he sat down for them. He slurped a little and champed noisily. His teeth were starting to give him trouble. He swallowed the last of the cup, belched and got the daily news delivered to him via Aparna.

The price of fish was atrocious, the quality abysmal. The onions were getting worse by the day and she had never seen a potato crop that poor. She couldn't understand that. The monsoons had been good. It was probably all the middlemen, hoarding the good stuff to sell to the rich. The poor people like them were left with the residue.

Tapas listened as he usually did, with a hem and a haw, and a harrumph at regular intervals.

Tea consumed and news absorbed, Tapas brought out his tablas. He was just warming up when Kunal arrived with his guitar case. As Tapas played a few tentative beats, Kunal tuned his guitar. Then as Tapas broke into a steady rhythm, Kunal backed him with his flatpicking style and odd chord shapes. They broke off often, picking up and resetting and restarting with many nods, smiles and exclamations.

This is the time of the day that Tapas liked best. The job was a job, this was life itself. They played for about an hour. Halfway through, Aparna disappeared into the tiny kitchen to set about preparing the evening meal. Finally, Kunal set his guitar aside and the two sat and chatted. They flicked the ash from their cigarettes over the porch into the street; there was no ashtray in the house.

Kunal picked up his case and left for his dinner and Aparna appeared to tell Tapas to put away the tablas and wash up for dinner.

After dinner, Tapas sat down to watch TV, Aparna by his side. The soap opera went through about fifteen climactic moments in the twenty minutes of airtime allotted to it between the main focus of the show, a series of advertisements selling everything from TVs to underwear.

Then the lights were turned out and Tapas Paul, the conductor and his wife, Aparna, slept.

Tapas dreamed of Saturday nights, when the train didn't run. He was on stage, his bandmates around him and he was playing, living, being the tablas, oblivious to the audience that had magically appeared, cut off from a life that offered him tragedy in the past, little in the present and nothing more for the future.

Aparna dreamed of her life in the tiny town in the countryside where she had grown up.

The little pond, where the daily gossip was exchanged among squeals of merriment. She dreamed of the brief moments of joy and the years of grief as she held the tiny warm and then cold bodies in her arms, her tears of momentary joy mixing into a century of sorrow.

Retribution

Dermot heard the wail of fire engines racing through the streets of Liverton. The windows of the café had burst open and the flames licked the walls outside.

The flames competed with the smoke for ascendancy. The fire engines, two of them, came to a stop in the square. Firemen jumped out and set up to fight the flames. They seemed not to be in a hurry, but this was deceptive. With practised ease and efficiency, they soon had a stream of water aimed directly at the heart of the fire.

Steam joined the flames and smoke. The middle of the building was burning furiously and as he watched, it gave way and the house seemed to cave inwards. The pressure of the water on the weakened beams was too much and the little café collapsed inwards into itself.

The couple standing there watched the destruction of their café. Lily stamped her feet in frustration, her body taut as she screamed obscenities into the wind. Her husband, Willy, watched the flames and smoke without seeming to see them, with one arm around Lily, trying, without success to calm her down.

Liverton was a small town and it suited Willy perfectly. It allowed him to get away from London, where "fine dining" basically meant high energy requirements from the staff in the kitchen.

Aunt Lucy's death came at a time when he was burnt out and ready to quit. The money she left Willy, together with the cottage, allowed him to convince Lily to leave the rush of London behind and move to the more tranquil surroundings on the edge of Dartmoor.

Lily's experience as a business consultant came in handy as they scoured the area for a suitable restaurant. The pub in Liverton had been shut down the year previously. It helped that it was just ten minutes away from their new home in Aunty Lucy's cottage in Bovey Tracey.

Dermot took up the challenge and converted it into a café to serve the steady stream of hikers, visitors and tours that passed through Liverton. The café had served breakfast, lunch sandwiches and tea to tourists and daytrippers headed for Hay Tor and Dartmoor. Lily, drawing upon her experience in marketing, had convinced Willy that catering to the niche market would serve them well. The townsfolk would not be that willing to buy sandwiches that they could make at home. Instead, they would leverage the tourist traffic that went through town, heading for the walks and hikes in the countryside. Willy had agreed. After the last few years turning out "gourmet" meals in London, this gave him the ability to relax, while still doing what he had wanted to do, serve up meals to customers.

The sandwiches were good, the coffee was excellent. Willy was starting to branch out into handcrafted fruit based drinks, which were starting to become well known.

The name, Lily & Willy, had been Lily's idea, too. Willy was too busy working on the renovations to care about the name. For two years, their little café supplied basic food to travelers. The local populace also appeared every once in a while.

Now, as they watched in anguish, their dreams went up in smoke.

Dermot, the cause of the fire, reached the top of the hill, shrugged off his pack and sat down. He had a clear view of the village below him.

He had been a cook at Lily and Willy for six months. He had always found the name of the café stupid. He got that it was the names of the two who owned it, but Lily & Willy? Seriously! Good riddance to it. That would teach them to accuse Dermot of slacking on the job.

Six months Dermot had fried eggs, made omelettes, sliced bread and ham, wrapped sandwiches and made sure the coffee was ready. All through that time, he had never stopped dreaming of Rose.

Very early, Lily had spoken with Willy and told him to keep Dermot away from customers.

"He's just not good with people. Let him stick to the kitchen. I can handle the front, and you can help as well, being the middleman between the customers and that kid."

"He's not a bad kid, actually."

Willy was too preoccupied with the suppliers and supplies, the preparation methods and the general running of the business to care about Dermot's lack of social skills. He was grateful that he had the extra pair of hands in the kitchen to take care of the basic tasks that required little by way of thought once Willy had the setup taken care of.

Lily was sceptical.

"I don't trust him. There's something broken in there. He's not normal."

"Ah, leave him be! Poor kid!"

"I'd watch him, Will, really, that guy isn't fully there."

Dermot had hated every moment of his time in the little kitchen of Lily & Willy. He hated Rose for forcing him to leave Camden Town. He couldn't understand what he had done to be kicked out of her life. He hated Willy for not standing up to Lily. Most of all he hated Lily for not trusting him, for never letting him slack, for always being there to make sure he was doing the work.

Dermot wanted to dream of Rose, but Lily was always there to harass him. Rose; he wanted to go back to Rose. Tomorrow, he would go back and see Rose. He could go back to working at the little store again. They'd been sorry to see him go. They'd be glad to get him back.

Rose, too, would know what a mistake she had made to make him go away.

He flipped open the matchbook and counted the matchsticks. There were three left.

He turned and walked away down the other side of the hill. Five miles down in the glade below, he wrapped himself up in his sleeping bag and slept.

He awoke as the dawn's early light slowly brightened the sky. He packed up and left down through the woods. The 8:07 bus deposited him an hour later in the town of Newton Abbot, fifteen minutes walk to the rail station.

In Liverton, the next morning, Lily did most of the talking as the townsfolk gathered on the street to commiserate and find out more of what happened.

"I'm sure that creep had something to do with this. We had to fire him. He was unable to keep up, he was always dreaming of something and he would mess up orders on a regular basis. Now he's disappeared. So, of course, I think he did this. Why would he vanish like that?"

The police had set up a bulletin asking for information about a Dermot Webster, 22 years old. There was a photograph attached, a grainy, photo that could have been anyone.

Dermot arrived in Camden Town by noon and was at Rose's house by 12:30. He stood there a moment, looking around the street. It was a familiar street, yet strange street. Nothing had seemed to change, yet he felt that everything had.

She wasn't home. The door was locked and there didn't seem to be anyone there. Dermot realized she'd still be at the library where she worked.

Across the street was the teashop where they had sat so many times. He sat at a table by the window for more than an hour, his bag next to him. He had a sandwich and a tea. The missed breakfast and the sparse dinner the night before had caught up with him.

He wandered out into the streets and found himself in a park. He lay down on the grass, his bag serving as his pillow. The sun was warm and the breeze was gentle. The clouds were merely wispy strands in the blue, clear sky.

He was back at the teashop at five, taking up his vigil from the same table he had left hours ago. His cup of tea lay untouched in front of him.

They arrived, hand in hand.

She wore a flowery, summery dress. Her companion was tall, had a mop of fair hair and a trace of facial hair. He watched her take out the key from her bag, unlock the door and kiss him. They went in, his arm around her waist.

"We're closing now. Would you like to pay now?"

He looked up at lady who was standing there watching him look out at the happy couple.

"Oh, yes. I'll just pay cash."

He left with his head full of thoughts that seemed to rush this way and that. He walked out to the station and stood there leaning against the wall of the ticket office. The evening rush swirled past him. He slumped to the floor, unaware of the legs that rushed by him, the voices that came and went, voices that could not drown out the voices in his head.

She had to pay. She had deserted him. Rejected his love, his adoration, and she had to be punished.

He put his hand in his pocket and felt the reassurance of the matchbook. He didn't have access to the kitchen and the flammables there, like he had in Liverton. He'd have to buy something.

That night, the fire in Camden Town was sudden. Before it was successfully put out, it had destroyed one home and caused the residents of the two downwind to be evacuated.

The house was now a mass of smoking embers. The bodies recovered from the embers were charred beyond recognition.

Dermot dosed against the wall of the station in Camden Town. He took the first bus out to Paddington and by 8 AM, he was on the train.

Bodmin Moor was a large and lonely place. He remembered tales of escaped convicts, hiding in the deserted crags and tors. He could stay there, unknown, unseen, away from the fuss and bother he had left behind in Liverton and, now, in Camden Town.

He bought himself a sandwich and started the long walk into the Moor itself. It was past dusk as he rolled out his bed in the lee of a tor. He sat there, the matchbook in his fingers twirling as he looked out into the darkness.

There were two matchsticks left.

He slept fitfully. Images of Rose in a pan with eggs, crying out to him flashed through his mind, interspersed with images of Lily yelling at him to hurry up.

He woke up to find a face looking down at him. It was cragged with lines, sported grey strands of hair that grew outwards, hiding the mouth and approaching the eyes. The hair was just as grey and scraggly under a wool cap, with eyebrows that seemed to overshadow the hollows of the eyes.

"And who would you be? What you doing here?" said the face.

Dermot struggled up and saw the wiry figure encased in boots, a ragged coat, and pants that hadn't seen a wash in a while.

"Well?" said the voice.

It was rough, muffled under the effect of the facial hair.

"I'm a camper. I came last night."

"Oh, a camper. Fancy that! This is my land. Get off my land."

"I thought this was part of the open Moor. Doesn't belong to anyone."

The old man stared at him.

"Got any food? Give it to me", he said.

Dermot stood up, opened his pack of sandwiches and offered them to the old man.

"Yeah, now we're talking. Now, shut up while I eat."

Dermot was incapable of thought. He stood up and walked a few steps, beating his chest to counter the chill of the morning air. He took in the old man.

AJESH SHARMA

The old man was demolishing the sandwiches, taking great big bites, his cheeks bulging. He took out a large and very shiny knife and cut open the apple. Dermot watched the knife.

"You're a good lad," said the old man, bits of half chewed apple spraying from his mouth. He pointed his knife at Dermot, as he spoke, sharp thrusts that built a sense of unease in Dermot.

"This is a lonely country. Nobody comes here. Why are you here? This is my land."

"I thought this was free land."

"Free? You call it free, huh? Let me tell you what freedom means, lad! It means, not having to talk to people. It means, not paying for your food. Food, and all them taxes!. Free land. My land and don't you forget it!"

Dermot took an involuntary step back.

"I didn't know I was trespassing. I'm sorry. I'll leave now."

The old man snorted and got up. He towered over Dermot. His knife flashed at Dermot as he spoke.

"Leave? Where do you think you'll go! This is all there is, lad! You think you can run away? What are you running away from?"

"I didn't do anything", Dermot whispered.

The old man roared, his head thrown back so Dermot could see the lines of dirt that passed for wrinkles along the neck.

"Oh, yes, you did! You're running away from something you did! How bad was it? Was it as bad as what I did?"

"I don't know what you did. I didn't do anything."

"Come, lad! Don't bother lying. Not to me. I killed a rich man. I killed his wife and then I killed him. That's what I did, see?"

Dermot took another step back, his eyes wide as the knife in the old man's hand gleamed in the early morning rays of the sun.

"He stole my work from him, didn't he, the sly bastard. The judge agreed with him. Let me tell ya, lad, don't trust the judges. The lawyers lie because they like to and the judges favour the rich man. Because they get paid by the rich man, don't they? Yeah, I was left with nothing. So I killed his wife, because he wasn't home yet. Then I waited for him to come home, and I killed him. With this very knife!"

The old man eyed him, his eyes seeming to drill through Dermot's brain into his thoughts.

"Well, what did you do? Come on, out with it!"

So Dermot told him what he had done. He didn't look up as he talked. He didn't dare see the old man, his knife or catch the expression on his face.

The old man listened intently, until Dermot's voice faded away in a faint sob. For a moment, the two remained frozen, still, intent.

Finally the old man spoke. There was a sad timbre to his voice.

"You destroyed the business of those people because you didn't like them. And you killed those two poor innocent young people who did you no harm. I killed because they stole my life from me. You killed innocent people because you felt slighted. It's not the same, lad. It's not the same."

He pulled out his knife, and stood there poised.

"I can't have you on my land. Did you hear me? I can't have that evil on my land! I'm more than enough here. I can't have you as well!"

A dull ache seemed to start at the back of Dermot's head. He fell to the ground and lay there, at the old man's feet. A flash of light through the fading light was the last thing he saw, as he felt a searing pain across his neck and then he knew no more.

AJESH SHARMA

The old man rifled through his bag and found a little tent, a gas stove with a tank and the matchbook.

Two weeks later, a group of hikers reported their discovery of the charred remains of a campsite and a half burned body.

On a rock nearby, was a small structure made with rocks. Balanced inside was a single matchstick.

The Angler on the Credit

He hummed a quiet tune, as he parked his car and carried out his gear to the riverbank. It was gathering dusk in late October. The air was chilly and would the temperatures, he knew, would go down a few degrees as the last of the sun fell below the horizon completely.

He suddenly became aware of someone watching him. He turned and nodded at the man, who was watching with curiosity and mild amazement as he brought out all his fishing rods, boxes of tackle and bait and arranged it all around him on the little wooden platform off the banks of the Credit River, on the other side of the lighthouse on Lakeshore Avenue.

"Is this a better place to catch fish than out in the lake?"
"Yes, you get trout, plenty of them, some are nice and big"
"It's already past 6 pm. How long will you fish?"
"Till the morning"
"You fish all night?"
"Oh yes. It's very peaceful."
"Do you mind if I ask you more questions? I'm curious and I find it quite interesting that you're here in Canada, given that, like me you're from the Indian subcontinent."
"You are from India?"

"Yes. And you're from Pakistan or Bangladesh?"

"Bangladesh."

"If you don't mind, I'd like to sit and watch you. Maybe, you can tell me how you got here, why you like to fish."

"It is ok."

"You will fish all night? What about your family?" asked the Indian.

"Oh, she divorced me. Now I fish," he said, as he settled in with finality, with ease.

As the temperatures fell, the two men sat there talking.

"My name is Shakib. I come from a town. You know it? Chittagong."

"Ah, Chattogram."

"Yes. You know Bengali? You are from Kolkata?"

"I spent many years there. Learned a little Bengali."

"I used to be fisherman, there. Now I'm fisherman here. See. Same."

"How did you get to Canada? From fisherman to taxi driver is a long trip!"

"You want to hear my life history?"

"Hain. Please. Aami shunte chai. *(I want to listen.)*"

And so the Bangladeshi taxi driver, sitting down to fish on the Credit River, in Canada, told the Indian his story.

The Indian, who was learning to write, heard it and wrote this story as he thought it should be told.

Shakib knew all about hunger and hard work.

When he was old enough to go on the daily fishing trip with his father, he quickly came to understand what it meant to have his hands rubbed raw. He came back from the daily sail his muscles aching knowing that the job was only half done. They still had to lay the fish out in the market, entice the customers, indulge in intense bargaining, to make the very bare minimums required to keep body and soul together for one more day for the family.

He was already aware that there was no escape from the circle of their daily life.

This was the only life Shakib knew. They left at dawn in their little boat, father and eldest son. Just like his father had gone out with his father before him.

There were four of them in the family now. Zubair, the youngest, was not quite old enough to accompany them, but he was old enough to sort and spread out the daily catch on the blue plastic sheet that served as their store in the little fish market. Zubair it was who packed the fish for the customer after the haggling process was completed.

His father conducted the haggling with skill tinged with just a trace of resignation. He had never really recovered from the shock of Nazia's death. Nazia had borne him three children, two of them boys. Nazia had never complained, never raised her voice and never shed a tear. Nazia had gone about her work with no trace of feeling. Nazia had died as she had lived, quietly, without complaint.

There was little time for the family to grieve; the daily cycle of fishing, selling, cleaning up and cooking before a dreamless sleep saw to that. Saliha had taken over the kitchen after that, moving seamlessly into a role for which she had so far been apprentice to her mother.

Life was as it could be for a poor fishing family in Bangladesh. Shakib's duties in the house also included cleaning and helping Saliha cook their daily meal. He was responsible for grinding the spice paste for her, fetching and carrying and watching her cook; guiding her, though she was already able to handle the simple meals they ate. Shakib's father would sit outside their little semi permanent shack, with the faded tarpaulin that served as rain proofing, smoking a chain of *beedis*, small hand rolled cigarettes, staring into the distance, his mind blank, not daring, after many years of practice, to think of anything. Especially not a future that was any different from the present.

Saliha would soon be looking after another household. He needed to find someone willing to take her on, as wife, childbearer, and housekeeper.

Life around them was changing, though it had not yet made any inroads into their lives. Bigger trawlers were slowly taking over the fishing fleet. Smaller independent fishermen like him were losing out to the bigger and faster ships with winches and other mechanical devices to reduce the load and increase the catch.

Shakib's father saw the change around him and was silent, resigned to his life. He expected nothing and was prepared to take life as it came to him. In any case, he had no power to effect any change.

When the owner of one of the big trawlers came to visit, the decision that came to be was the biggest this small family had ever had had to make.

Shakib watched his father's reluctant acquiescence to the offer. It was painful to observe. There was a touch of apathy, almost, in the way he capitulated to the offer. Shakib was aware that he was resigned to his fate. Life for Moinul, widower to Nazia, father of Shakib, Saliha and Zubair, hadn't been one of choices that he had the power to make. This was just another piece of life thrown at him.

At 20, Shakib was leaving to start a new life. He was going to see places he had never seen or heard of before. He little knew just how far he was going to go.

For the next three years, Shakib was busier than he remembered. Work on the trawler was harder than even his life at home.

He started out in the kitchen, and graduated to mending nets, as he learned to use the devices. The raw physical exertion of the final haul of the heavy nets the winch had brought up to the side and the sorting at almost frantic speed left him exhausted at the end of the day.

The pay was better, though, and Shakib was able to set a little bit aside and send some back to his father.

Three months after he started, he moved out of the house and took up a shared bed space nearer the trawler. The evening meal was cooked, eaten and cleaning up done in record time before sleep overtook Shakib's body and mind.

Soon he developed an easy relationship with the others on the boat. The fishing village was also changing. Heavy demand for shrimp and pomfret from foreign markets was driving up prices. Trawler operators were quick to capitalize on this newfound revenue stream. There were new faces to be seen in the village and money, more money than the village had ever seen. Ashore, his circle of acquaintances grew slowly.

On days off, the trawler crews often banded together and headed across the bay to the big town. This was a real seaport with big ships that crossed the oceans to faraway lands.

Used to the compact utility of the trawler, Shakib was at first excited by the size of the ships. The ship folk seemed better dressed, seemed to have far more money to spend. Shakib, could not but help compare the way they carried themselves, with a near swaggering assurance, to the trawler crews.

These trips became a regular fascination with him. He took to going over whenever he had a chance. The sailors he met told tales of far away lands; the women, the shops, the bright lights until Shakib wanted nothing more than an opportunity to see and experience these for himself.

It took him some time to approach the sailor working near one of the large ships. He eased up to him and casually asked "What kind of fish do you catch in that?"

The sailor looked up, saw him, shrugged and said, "We don't catch fish. We carry all kinds of cargo across the seas."

He waited, then slyly looked at Shakib.

"You want to see what it looks like inside?"

Shakib nodded.

"Yes, I'd very much like to see".

From the moment he stepped on board, Shakib, wanted to stay there. He wished he could find a way to be on this ship. The next few hours went by in a blur.

Years later, he could not say how it happened. When he put his thumbprint on the contract, it was done.

He was no longer a fisherman. The next day he packed his few belongings and went to visit his father. His father had aged 15 years in the last 3 years. Saliha was married and had left the house. He was alone with Zubair. They were doing the work of 3 people between them.

Shakib was conscious of a feeling of shame as he handed over the bulk of his savings to his father. He told him he was going away on the big ships across the bay. He would visit often. He would send money.

They both knew what would happen. Neither could catch the other's eye and then Shakib was gone. Gone to the big ships. Gone away from fish. Gone away from the life he knew.

He settled into the merchant ships. The long hauls across the sea took him to Indonesia, Australia and China and even further away.

One fine day, Shakib found himself steaming through the mouth of the St Lawrence River into Quebec City. Two days after docking, Shakib found himself suddenly jobless.

The shipping company, faced with mounting losses, could no longer run the ship. Shakib was left with no way to go home. Luckily, for him, one of the crew had been to Quebec before and had Bangladeshi connections in the city. Shakib found himself living with a Bangladeshi family he had never seen before, while he tried to work out what his options were.

Three months were enough to tell him that he would do better away from Quebec. He'd had a hard time picking up some elementary English, but French was beyond him. The Bangladeshi dockworker he shared a room with told him he'd be better off in Toronto. He knew someone who could help Shakib get the right papers.

So Shakib went to Toronto and got a job in a restaurant. A small eatery that advertised itself as serving Indian food, Shakib found his experience with fish was deemed useful, though he had much to learn about cooking and serving.

He spent a year living with a taxi driver, in a little apartment off Danforth Avenue, above a small, crowded convenience store. In the summer evenings, he, the taxi driver and the taxi driver's friends would sit outside the store, sipping tea, swapping stories, smoking, often reminiscing of the days in the old country. The store owner joined them sometimes on days when business was slow.

Thrown into the company of taxi drivers, Shakib soon found himself learning how to drive and became, inevitably, a taxi driver. The network helped with the work permit, the licence and then permanent residence.

Driving in Toronto, Shakib's English improved. He enrolled in ESL classes and gained confidence every passing day.

News from Bangladesh was rare and sometimes grim. Monsoon flooding had taken his father and Zubair. Their bodies were never found.

Shakib was too far removed to figure out what he should have felt. He'd grown up in a small fishing village in Bangladesh and folks there worked hard, lived philosophically, got on with the day to day work needed to eat and to live. Saliha had three children to look after, with a husband who worked in the docks of Chattogram.

That was the summer that Shazia came to Toronto.

She was second cousin to the owner of the convenience store. She was young, and was visiting Canada, in the hope of finding a match or job, whichever came first.

The storeowner had seen the potential of getting his cousin out of Bangladesh. Shakib was right there, just a couple of years older than her. The storeowner saw Shakib as dependable and hardworking. He had seen him grow from a diffident newcomer to an experienced taxi driver.

The marriage lasted 12 years.

In those years, Shakib wished for nothing more than escape from his life.

She was at complete odds with his easy going, take it as it comes approach to life. She came from a small town and she'd been to the big city. She was in Toronto and there was much to see and do here. She wanted to go out. She wanted to go for holidays. She wanted him to stop smoking. His attempts at pleasing her were half hearted, easily seen as such.

It gave her a harder edge. With help from the network and the Shazia's cousin, they put a down payment on an apartment in Scarborough, but she wasn't happy with his status of taxi driver.

"Why can't you get another job? This taxi thing is fine for a bachelor."

"I don't have any other skills. What do you want me to do?"

"Why not take some computer classes and apply for a call centre?"

Shakib could not imagine himself in an office. He liked driving taxis. He met different people and it gave him some freedom, a semblance of his former life. He enjoyed meeting the other taxi drivers, sharing a smoke in the parking lots, waiting for a fare, exchanging gossip, drinking tea.

The divorce, when it came, was a relief for him and her.

She got the apartment, naturally, and Shakib decided to move out of the area completely.

He found a shared rental in an apartment building on Paisley Boulevard in Mississauga, away from his old friends, haunts and memories. He continued to drive a taxi. Finally, in his late 40s, Shakib was at ease.

There was nothing for him in his shared apartment. The furniture was barebones, a simple TV with a subscription to Asian channels was the only luxury.

AJESH SHARMA

His co-residents had nothing in common with him. There was no background, no sentiments, and no shared stories. The communal smoke and hot chai sessions in Scarborough were a distant memory.

He indulged himself by going back to his roots, fishing for trout and bass in season; fishing for pleasure.

He settled in to a regular routine of driving by day and angling in the Credit River by night. Out on the riverbank he was alone, but he was relaxed. Most days he met no one, but when he did meet other anglers, they kept the code, nodding acknowledgement and settling into their own private worlds with rod and line.

It was not perfect, but life was never going to be perfect. He had learnt that lesson a long, long time ago, handling the boat, the nets, and the work back in the little village on the outskirts of Chattogram. He hadn't been happy in the past, back when he lived with his mother, father and his younger sister and brother. He knew that now.

He was now no longer Shakib, the fisherman, Shakib, the deck hand in the merchant navy, Shakib, the taxi driver, Shakib, the failed husband.

He was the happy, peaceful, easy going, Angler on the Credit.

Closure

He found his attention wandering to the time on the corner of the screen. She'd be here by 11am.

"They", he corrected himself.

He'd woken up at 6 am as usual, telling himself it was just a regular day as he went through his morning routine; take the dog for a walk, finish a mild jog, organize breakfast of coffee and toast. Now he sat in his office, his computer screens in front of him, he settled down to write his usual morning piece, but found himself scrolling up and down and through the news, which, as per usual were disconcertingly catastrophic.

He gave up his attempt at writing, wandered back in to the kitchen, and poured himself some orange juice. He drank it as he stared out of the window at the poolside patio, not really registering what he was seeing. From the fridge, he took out the chicken kebabs he'd been marinating since last night. He checked through all the items he'd planned for the lunch and decided he'd may as well chop up the salad ingredients and keep it ready for the dressing.

"Keep busy", he told himself.

He wondered why she was coming to see him.

He already knew about the upcoming wedding. She didn't need to drive up to see him in person. But she'd always taken her kids seriously and their daughter's wedding would be enough reason for her.

He finished shrinkwrapping the salad, and walked over to his study, sat down and wrote steadily for an hour, before he was interrupted by the phone.

"Hey, hi there! You on your way?"

He kept his voice even, careful to display no emotion that could be felt down the wire.

"Hey, yeah, we're coming off the ramp now, so I guess another thirty minutes or so?"

"Yeah, about twenty minutes or so. Call me when you reach the gate and I'll let you in. See you in a bit".

She sounded just as she had sounded over so many conversations over the years, thirty years. Thirty!

He sat there for a few moments, letting the enormity of that time sink in, the memories, the conversations. Very briefly, he held his head in his hands, then shook himself up, and walked over to the big overstuffed chair sitting in the corner of his study, over to his right. He took the cover off it, folded it and put it away in the closet. He dusted an imaginary speck of dust off the chair and stood there inspecting it.

It sat there, uncovered for the first time since it had been delivered and installed in his study.

He walked back to the patio, setting up the shade, moving the lounge chairs around to get them out of the direct sun of the cloudless California sun. He loved the rolling hillsides, the vineyards in the distance. Ever since his first visit, he'd wanted to live here. With five successful books behind him, and the proceeds from the sale of his share in the consulting business, the small estate just west of Napa had finally become possible.

The last couple of years had been spent in modifying, upgrading and putting the images in his head into the house.

The phone rang.

"Hi, how do you open the gate?" she asked.

"Hang on a sec".

He walked over to the panel in the wall, could not stop himself checking the video screen, then pressed the button.

"Thanks", she said, as the car drove in.

He walked out to the patio, the golden retriever padding along with him. He stood on the porch watching the drive. The big Golden Retriever, sat upright next to him, tongue out, tail still, waiting. Waiting for the car, for her.

He watched her get out and wave to him. He waved back. She was smiling, a smile he knew so well.

He smiled back and walked down the porch stairs as she came up. The hug felt familiar but slightly uncomfortable. Behind her came her companion. He hadn't been able to think of him as her husband. They shook hands, not being able to hug despite the long years of friendship they took back to their collective days in university.

"Come on in. How was the drive up? Did you have any trouble with the directions?"

She straightened from petting the golden retriever and said "No, you always prided yourself on your directions and these were always perfect!"

Her smile took the sting out of it. She was trying, he saw, which amused and surprised him a little.

"Alright, Rex. Give her some space!"

Rex, his tail wagging frantically, turned to look at him and then went back to her.

"Oh, what a lovely doggie! What's your name, then? Rex? Oh you're a handsome lad!"

"He's three years old. Likes people."

In his head, the words "unlike me" flashed through.

"You guys want a drink? Wine or beer? I have some lemonade, too. The wine comes from the vineyard over there".

He pointed back across the slope where the vineyard stretched out.

"We specialize in sweetish whites, rieslings, mostly. Come on out to the back, it's nice out".

He left them seated and went back in to get the drinks, riesling for her, beer for him. They chatted about the view from where they sat.

"So you made it! You're a famous author! You sold the business, as well. How does it feel to be retired and rich?" she said.

"It's nice to know your phone isn't going to ring with someone else's problems. Relaxing!"

"Are you working on another book? When is that coming out?"

"Oh, I don't know, it's been a hard grind getting this one down. It seems I said everything I wanted to say in the first two so I'm going back to being lazy and taking my time. It's going to be different from the others, I think."

Steve said, "I read them, too. You've got a gift".

"Thanks! I just write down whatever comes, good to know it makes some sort of sense for others."

They talked about various things as he busied himself with getting the lunch. They sat there, eating, drinking, chattering easily.

He wondered when she'd get to the reason for coming to see him.

She insisted on helping with the clearing up. In the kitchen, she said, "I wanted to talk to you about a couple of things".

She turned to Steve and said, "Will you please wait here while I finish?"

She turned and said, "Is there someplace we can talk?"

"Follow me", he said.

They walked into the library and he gestured to one of the two easy chairs there. They sat and she took a deep breath.

"This is difficult, but I want to speak with you directly. I did not want to do this over the phone."

"Hey, I know that Andrea is engaged. I assume this has something to do with that?"

"Yes. She wants you to attend the wedding and I wanted to know how you felt about it."

"Hmm, well, here's the thing. Does she really want me to be there? Does she want her Dad there? Or is she wanting to keep up appearances? Or is it the successful author she wants to show off? You know, Andrea has always been focused on herself. After that last time, five years ago, she did not seem keen on telling people she had a father. So I'm confused by this."

"You know that she cares, deeply. She's always wanted you to give her attention and you never had time for her"

He was silent, not wanting to rush into the gap. He did not want to start that discussion all over again.

"Did she send you? Or was it your idea?"

"It was my idea. The kids both care for you, they always have. You were just not able to see it. And I know you've always cared deeply for them and they were not able to see it too. I've talked to both of them and"

Her cut her off.

"Sorry, I know all that. But they are adults and they should start behaving like it. I was always being told I did not treat them as adults and now they need to start living it."

She sat back and stared at the ceiling. He waited.

"So what do you want to do?"

"I want Andrea to call me. I want to talk to her. I want to hear what she really wants. I'm really tired of the kids using you as their mouthpiece. I'm never sure whether what I'm hearing is what you want or they want. This has to stop. Now."

"They're scared of you. They don't want to hurt you. You have to know that. You do know that."

"Phyllis, you know exactly what I'm saying. You know more about me before I know it myself. You've always known. I think you've pandered to them. Even now, you are protecting them and I don't think they need protection. Not from me. Frankly, I find it insulting. They need to have a direct line to me. That's the reason we're having this conversation. That's the reason you …" He stopped, shook his head and sat back.

"So this is not going anywhere, then?"

"Yes, I'm afraid so, Phyll. There comes a time when you have to stop running and make a stand. I made my stand and I live here all by myself. I have some income, enough to afford this house. I do what I've always wanted to do. I have no one to share it with and it does bother me sometimes, but I know, that that is not something I will have now. I've come to terms with my life, Phyll. If you ask me whether I'm happy, I'll have to say, I'm as happy as I can be given the circumstances. That is enough."

"So you're happy, really happy?" she leaned forward, looking at him with enquiring eyes.

"As happy as I can be. What about you, though? Are you happy?"

She paused before she said, "I'm well looked after. I have everything I need."

They sat back and stared at each other. The silence seemed to last too long.

"Yes, I can see that. You've moved on, I see, and I hope you're happy. You certainly looked happy at Mark's wedding. At least, in the photos I saw, because I never got an invitation to that wedding. Thanks for the photographs, by the way. At least I did get to see my son on his wedding day. A couple of months later, but ..."

"I didn't think you'd be happy to attend."

"Assuming again? How come you didn't think that I would want to be invited to my son's wedding? Though in this case, you may have been right. I'd certainly not have been the happiest person there."

"So would you have come? If I'd invited you?"

"I don't know. I probably would have come. Did Mark ask about me?"

"Would it have mattered?"

"Whether Mark wanted me at his wedding? Whether my son wanted me at his wedding? You really do not understand, do you? I think this conversation is going exactly like all the other conversations in the past. So, let me look forward then. As you said, we can't turn time back, unless we can somehow make the earth spin the other way, very quickly, what, 12 times 365 days, give or take a leap day or two."

"Alex, I didn't come here to bring up all that. I'm sorry about shutting you out of Mark's wedding. I... I don't want that to happen again. I came here to ask you to please come for Andrea's wedding. I want you to give her away. It's a very simple thing."

"Simple? You think you can just call me and say you want to come over and then all you want is a simple yes to a request like this? Are you kidding me?

"Well, I wanted to see you personally. I know I messed up by not talking to you about Mark's wedding. I didn't want to make the same mistake again. Andrea needs someone to give her away."

"Does she want this? Don't you have anyone else to do that? Steve?"

"She wants you to give her away."

"Why don't you ask Andrea to call me? I want to talk to her. I want to hear what she really wants. I'm really tired of the kids using you as their mouthpiece. I'm never sure whether what I'm hearing is what you want or they want. This has to stop.

"They're scared of you. They don't want to hurt you. You have to know that. You do know that. You're angry and you have every right to be."

"Phyll, why don't you just not meddle. Let her decide for herself what she wants to do. Don't tell her what she should or should not do. Does she know you're coming up to see me?"

She shook her head. He threw his hands up.

"You came all the way here to see me. To tell me what I should do. You've decided what Andrea wants. For her."

"I'm sorry for bothering you. It must be quite a disruption our coming today."

"Not a disruption, Phyll, we've known each other a helluva long time. You are always welcome"

She caught the slight accent on the 'You' and she had to look away. She got up to hide the look on her face.

"I'll ask Andrea to call me, ok? But, it would mean a lot if you would give her away. For her. To me. Please?"

"Tell her to call me. Tell her you spoke with me and I do love her a lot. I always have. Tell her I said so and she can call me anytime she wants."

"Ok. That's settled. Show me around the house".

"Should we call in Steve? We just left him sitting there by himself."

"No, I want to see where you work. I want to see where you write. We can show him the rest of the house later."

He led her to the study. She looked around at the large table and the multiple monitors.

"Wow, how many monitors do you need?" She was laughing.

"So this is where the magic happens, huh? Where those fancy words come out?"

"Sort of. Sometimes I go out to the patio and work for a bit. But mostly I write in here. I like it. It is exactly how I've always wanted it".

She looked around the room and saw the chair in the corner. She turned around to look at him. He was looking at the chair. She stood there, motionless, silent tears running down her cheeks. He was the first to stir, reaching out for the box of tissues. Gently he wiped away her tears, then folded her in his arms.

One last time. Five minutes, five silent minutes, they stayed locked in that embrace. Then she broke free.

"We should go."

He waited for her to compose herself and they went out to where Steve was standing, gazing out over the rolling hills at a small red plane buzzing through the blue sky.

They went through the house, the library, the music room, walked out through the vineyards and the wine storage. Then it was time for them to go.

He held the door open for her as she got into the car. Shut it gently and stepped back.

He stood at the bottom of the porch, Rex sitting patiently next to him, watching them, her, drive away, then turned and walked to his study. He stood there for a moment, staring at the chair in the corner. Then he walked over to it and sat down. He'd always known that he would have to be the first person to sit in it.

He leaned back, stretched out, closed his eyes and slept.

The Lake

It was midday when the sun started to develop a shadow. No one noticed it at first. When the light started changing, the workers in the field paused and looked up to see the sun disappearing behind a black shade.

Terror gripped the village. The men hurried home from the fields, driving the cattle and dogs before them with increasing urgency as the curtain slowly covered the sun. Mothers dropped their chores, gathered the children and with shrill cries hurried indoors. Doors were slammed shut and windows closed. A fearful calm enveloped the village.

The unusual silence was broken by odd murmurings of the women and men in prayer. As the day grew darker, sobs and muffled cries could be heard among the chanting that grew steadily in volume from many of the rough houses that sat around the little square. The village lay for seven minutes in a shroud of fear, and the strange and ominous darkness of midday. No one dared to leave the house, the windows remained shut, the doors barricaded from the evil forces that seemed imminent.

Then the curtain across the sun started to pass and as the light grew stronger again, the sobs and cries died down until the village lay deathly still and quiet.

Then the shadow passed and the sun's rays appeared through the cracks of the wooden shutters. Not a sound was heard.

It took the first brave villager another twenty minutes to step out into the day. A shout rent the air, other villagers appeared. The wailing started again but this time interspersed with prayers of thanks. Some fell upon the earth and prayed. Others jumped and sang.

Then one of the women saw the pale, almost translucent waif, standing there naked just outside the village at the edge of the forbidden forest to the east.

Her eyes glowed like burning coal. Her dark hair lay over her shoulders and down below her waist in sharp contrast to the whiteness of her skin. She seemed to float, with steps that were airy and light. She stopped short of the villagers now gathered in the square.

A hush fell upon the crowd. The crowd stilled and once again, the village fell into silence. A strange electric air seemed to surround her. Children were dragged away by their mothers, and the windows and doors were shut.

The first hesitant questions were left unanswered. The men, confused and amazed, talked among themselves, trying to make sense of the nude phenomenon.

Finally, one of the men was sent away for bread and a robe. The girl reached out and took the bread with listless arms. She ignored the robe, turned and walked to the edge of the woods and was lost in the dense trees.

That evening the village folk did nothing more than the very basic items needed for supper. Children remained indoors and only the bravest men stood on guard as dusk fell.

She would appear once a day at noon. This regularity helped mothers shelter the children from this daily naked appearance. The villagers learned to leave some food outside for her; bread, with cheese or corn, sometimes a piece of ham.

She spoke not a word. She did not respond to questions about her birth, whence she had come and why she had appeared. The villagers learned to offer no work to her. She would pick up the food and disappear into the woods in silence.

At first, the women would watch for her. They made some attempt to talk, but were rewarded with silence. Soon, they learned to simply leave the food out and go about their chores. The men, their hours filled with the work in the fields, stopped caring about her.

Often in the evening, the men would chatter about the legends. As the glasses of mead and rough beer were filled, emptied, and refilled, the tales would become more fanciful as the alcohol took effect.

The land had been cursed. This is why it had been without a monarch for such a long time. There were tales told of a wizard who controlled the destiny of the land. It was said that a king would appear, drawn by a magical power, understood and controlled by the wizard. No one seemed to know when that would happen.

The wizard was considered to be wise, his work, his intentions and his power over the land were beyond comprehension. He had never been seen. It was said that he would appear when the time was right, as would the king.

The villagers were well aware of an enchantment cast upon the woods to the east. In the middle of it, so the rumour went, stood a lake. It had once been connected to the river that now flowed half a mile away, from which the village drew its water.

It was said that the enchantment of the lake and its separation from the river was the work of the great, unseen wizard. The lake lay hidden by the tall trees that heightened the sense of foreboding.

No villager ever ventured into the woods. None of them had even seen the lake. It lay as in a fairy tale, a myth. Over time, the stories grew of its magical powers, powers not meant for the common man. It was believed the lake belonged to the wizard and the power of the lake would remain unlocked until he appeared.

On moonlit nights, the pale, strange naked one would sit by the lake and wait with unseeing eyes. At the first hint of the morning light, she would head to the little clearing where her bed of leaves would hold her in warmth as she slept till noon, when she walked to the village to pick up the bread that lay waiting for her. The time was chosen, but it had not yet come. She knew not when it would come or how it would reveal itself. She knew only that it would come and would reveal itself.

And so, she waited.

Winters came and went. Men and women worked and died, and their children grew up and started work in the farms and the homes, like their mothers and fathers before them. Yet her time had not yet arrived.

It was in the fall that the villagers saw the full moon and as they watched, a dark hand appeared to shade it.

That was the day a strange power drew her to the edge of the lake. She felt a strange tremor that came and went. She was compelled by one who held the knowledge of all that was to come to the spot which was chosen.

She sat with her toes just short of the pebbles that lead to the water, staring out into the distance, motionless and as still as the world surrounding her.

She'd watched the sun going down. Undulating colors now shimmered across the surface as the moon beamed down upon the lake. Across, on the far shore, a darkness rose up into the sky. Not a whisper of a zephyr dared disturb the serenity of the scene. As the full moon grew dark and the moments passed, she sat there, still as ever, waiting for her date with destiny.

Moments passed until the moon flickered and became brighter. A gentle breeze, barely a hint of air, grew stronger. A shaft of whiteness lit the path in front of her. Through the light appeared a sword, a magnificent sword. A strange precious metal shone through the leather wrapped around the hilt. The guard was studded at either end with a ruby that glowed fiery red. The pommel gleamed white as a diamond can.

She knew her time had come. She stood up, her bare arms bathed by the luminescence of that soft but bright light. A cloak of white gossamer floated towards her, enveloping her in its gentle folds. A gentle breeze sprung up.

She grasped the enchanted sword and glowed her way into the light and down to the water.

She could not hesitate. Firm and steady steps took her into the water, deeper and deeper until the waters covered the tip of the sword. The light turned off and the wind was calm again. The full moon appeared again, casting a warm glow upon the land.

The lake remained still, its waters had neither rippled nor moved as the lady entered it. The moon was mirrored on its surface, a perfect harmony of light and water. The land slept.

In the weeks ahead, the villagers found the food left for the pale waif lay untouched. No one sighted her. She disappeared into time in the same magical way she had appeared.

The years passed. Nobles fought battles to seize control of the land, which remained without a king.

There were cycles of plenty, peace, war, and famine as she lay in the lake, waiting. The legend of the king and wizard grew stronger. Stories changed. It was said that the king would appear and an enchanted sword would mark him out.

The lake lay as it had for years, peaceful and quiet, home to The Lady of the Lake. Deep in its depths, she lived with the sword by her side, waiting for the arrival of the knight to fulfil the prophecy, and her destiny.

He would appear one day. He would be named Arthur. He would receive the gift of Excalibur from her and mark his rightful place as king of the land. He would carry Excalibur and ride away into a legend that would last a thousand years.

A Manhattan Tale

Eckstein was lonely, they said. Eckstein didn't think so. He was always busy, doing something that most people thought was doing nothing.

Jay Eckstein was forty two, and single, and this made people click their tongue and make sympathetic noises. In their book, loneliness, or being alone, was not a desirable way to be. In the early days, Eckstein would try and correct them. Eventually, he found a way to ignore the noise and go on doing what he was doing, alone as always.

The only person who didn't care whether Eckstein was lonely or not, was Howie. He would greet Eckstein every morning as Eckstein sauntered out to hail his morning cab.

"Morning, Mr. Eckstein. Off to make another movie? What's it going to be today? Love story? Body lotion commercial?"

"Dishwashers", said Eckstein.

"Ah well, someone's gotta tell the world what they do, eh, so may as well be you. Have a great day, Mr. Eckstein!"

Howie was close to eighty years old and would never have dreamed of calling the residents of the apartment building by their first names. Jay Eckstein always felt that was a good thing. It gave him the opportunity to be friendly with Howie, without losing the formality inherent in their relationship.

Howie said the same thing almost every morning. Except weekends. On weekends, Eckstein wouldn't come down till almost noon. He lay in, reading a book from start to finish, then ran a quick 20 minutes on the treadmill, before going back up to have coffee and toast with avocado spread in a mess over it. When the book had particularly annoyed him, he would use peanut butter instead of avocado.

That particular weekend when it all changed for Eckstein had started like every other weekend. Done with his morning routine, he stepped out into the street and sniffed the air. The smells of New York City mingled with the sounds of New York City, busy as always, with trucks loading or unloading cartons down the street, cabs and cars mingling with cyclists and avoiding the trucks.

He walked down to Chelsea, a leisurely twenty minute walk in the cool late spring air. Over his head, the sun played with the clouds, his shadow appeared and disappeared as he strolled along. As he reached The Kitchen, the sun disappeared completely. He shivered a bit and went in, as much to get out of the sudden nip in the air, as to reach a destination.

The Kitchen usually had some to interest him. This time, Paulina Olowska was being featured. There were no movies on the board for today. He liked the movies. They allowed him to indulge in flights of fancy away from his day job of carefully storyboarded commercials. Sometimes, he would take ideas back with him and try, usually unsuccessfully, to convince the marketing gurus to modify their carefully planned stories.

He wandered around the exhibits for a bit and decided he was hungry. He walked into Mokbar and took his Ribeye Bulgogi over to the bar looking out of the window into the street. He liked to watch life go by.

As he stirred his noodles, he wondered why he hadn't opted for the rice.

"Wishing you'd chosen rice, are you?"

"Huh? Sorry, are you talking to me?"

Eckstein turned to see the girl who had just parked herself in the chair on his right.

"Here, you can have mine, if you like. I'll swap. It's the same except, I got it with rice."

"Uh no! It's fine, fine. Don't worry about it. I was just..."

"Wishing it was rice. What made you pick noodles?

"Noodles are good. "

He appraised the girl. Two dangling gold earrings, a purple gash for lips, the only items of decoration in a pale, almost sallow complexioned face. The eyes were dark smoky black, the eyebrows unplucked. The hair was streaked in purple and pink highlights, tastefully done at the ends. She wore blue jeans and a pink cotton blouse tucked in.

He went back to his noodles, expertly using the chopsticks. He was dimly aware that the girl was just as expertly clicking the chopsticks as she made her way through her meal. The clicking bothered him. He wished she wouldn't feel the need to do that.

He finished his meal and sat back.

"How was it?"

"What?"

Eckstein swung his head to look at the girl.

"Oh it's good, I'm used to it. I come here all the time."

"This is the first time for me", she said.

They walked out together. The sun was back and the air was suddenly warmer.

"Well", she said, "good bye. Maybe we'll meet again here."

Eckstein made suitably polite noises and went back home.

His phone rang as he unlocked the door to his apartment. He threw his keys into the bowl on the table by the door, kicked the door shut and pulled out his phone.

"Yes, ma"

"Jay, it's your mother."

"Yes, ma, I know."

"Jay, why can't get you get a proper phone instead of that cell thing?"

"Ma, I told you. No one has a landline anymore."

"They cause cancer, Jay."

"Yes, ma. It's ok."

"Jay, I want you to listen to me."

"Do I have a choice, ma?"

"Now, Jay, don't you take that tone with me."

"What is it, ma? I'm busy."

"That's what I wanted to talk to you about. You keep saying you're busy."

"I am."

"When are you getting married? Find a nice girl?"

"Oh, come on, ma! We've been through this a million times."

"Now, you listen to me, Jay."

"Ma, I told you..."

"Ben, talk to your son. He's not listening to me."

Ben Eckstein came on the line.

"Now, son, you listen to your mother."

"Sure dad."

"Are you doing ok for money? I can send you a check. I'll send you a check."

"Dad, I don't need money. I have a good job."

In the background, Eckstein heard his mother's voice.

"What did he say? Does he need money? You must send him a check, Ben."

Shirley Eckstein came back on line.

"Now, Jay, your dad is going to send you some money. Don't worry."

"Ma, I don't need..."

"Jay, you won't believe who I had tea with yesterday."

"Aunt Esther."

"Yes. Your Aunt Esther. And you know what?"

"She has a friend who has a daughter?"

"Samuel's cousin from Albany, was visiting. He runs a clothing store. He has a partner, Ezra Shapiro."

"And Ezra has a daughter."

"Jay, don't be smart with me, young man! You know, it's time you found a nice girl and settled down."

"Ma, you call me every weekend to tell me about some girl."

"Why can't you be a good son to your mother, Jay? Everyone I know has kids who are married."

"Yes, ma."

"Now look, this girl Calista, they call her Cally. I think it's horrid to shorten a lovely name like Calista. Don't you think so?"

"It's a lovely name. Hey look, ma, sorry to cut you off, but I have a call coming in. Love you. Gotta go."

"Jay, wait."

Eckstein put his phone down on the counter and flung himself on the couch.

Over the next two weeks, a sense of foreboding seemed to hang over him. It was then that he decided to go back to Chelsea market. He took his bulgogi with rice and parked himself on the barstool facing the street. He sensed the seat next to him being occupied. He concentrated on his plate.

"I see you've switched to rice."

He looked up and smiled.

"Yes. I did, didn't I? And you're having the noodles."

"My name is Calista. My friends call me Cally."

"Jay."

"Your lunch, I don't want to keep you from it. I hate cold food."

Jay nodded a thanks, and concentrated on his plate. He carried the empty plate away to the bar where the empties were and came back to Cally.

She held out her empty plate to him and he repeated the visit.

"I normally have a soda after my meal. Can I buy you something?" he asked.

"That's very kind of you. I'll have a soda, too. What do you normally get?"

"Diet Coke. Is that ok?"

"Sure!"

Jay returned with two sodas and they walked out into the sunshine. Jay turned left and Cally followed. They walked in silence to the High Line.

Jay had time to notice with appreciation that her hair no longer had the highlights. Her purple lips were a dark pink. A light dress with little scarlet and pink pimpernels all over ended in white sneakers.

Jay motioned to the stairs leading up, and Cally stepped up and they walked down the High Line to the Whitney. He hesitated.

"You going to go in?" Cally said.

She looked up inquiringly at Jay.

"Yeah. I like modern art. You want to join me?"

"Hey, why not? It's a lovely sunshiny day, so let's spend it indoors."

"I usually spend about an hour or so. I find it refreshes me. If you like we can give it a miss."

"I've never been", she said, "You can show me around?"

When they came out it was close to 3pm.

"Ok, that was kind a fun!" laughed Cally.

"Glad you enjoyed it."

"What do we do next?"

"Uh, I usually walk down and get a coffee."

"I could do that. Do you have a regular place?"

"Grounded Coffee is about ten minutes away."

"Let's go! Then this girl can sit and rest her weary legs."

The late spring was turning into the first days of summer as Eckstein and Calista strolled up 9th Avenue.

He ordered dark roast, black with no sugar. She asked for a cappuccino. They settled down at a table outside.

"So Cally, what do you normally do on a weekend? Clearly, not the art galleries!"

"I like to walk around. Stare into shop windows. I'm not a big shopper. Window shopping is more my thing."

"Is that a relaxing activity for you?"

"Oh yeah! I mean, you can look at a display in the store window and imagine all sorts of things."

"Like what? Give me an example."

"See, you can try and visualise the people who might buy the thing you're looking at. Why did they buy it? What sort of value do they attach to it? Where or how they would use it. What kind of people are they? Do they have families? And so on and on. No limit!"

"That's an interesting way of looking at it."

"When you say 'interesting', do you mean boring or of interest?"

"You know, you are the most direct person I've met."

"And in your head you're trying to work out whether you like it or not."

Jay raised his cup to her, drained it and set it down very carefully. He put his fingers together and looked into her face before speaking.

"To answer your second question, I'm inclined to not being fully intimidated by your directness."

"Oh wow! So you like it, huh! Imagine!" she said.

"I didn't quite say that! But, you know, I could get used to it."

"I'm, what's the word they used to use back in the day, um flabbergasted. Oh yeah!"

She dipped her spoon into the cappuccino and sucked it.

Jay said, "To answer your first question, it is of interest to me. But first, I want to ask you a direct question."

"Go ahead! Today is International Direct Talking Day, as far as I am concerned."

"What do you do? I mean, for a living?"

"I write. Or try to. I've had a couple of pieces here or there. Working on a novel right now."

"Ah, that accounts for the observational based imagination at the shop window thing."

"Guilty, I guess."

"Now to explain why it is of interest to me, I make commercials. And I wonder, often, who watches them, how many use them as pee breaks and how many actually end up buying the stuff being advertised as a direct result of the commercial."

"So you're as dreamy as I am. Married?"

"No. You?"

"Of course not. You knew that already, didn't you?"

"The first name gave it away. Yeah."

When they left the coffee shop, Jay turned to Cally.

"Well, here we are. Thanks for the company. I have to get on home and run a few errands."

"Sure! I guess I better go and run some errands myself."

"See, I live alone and that means I have to do all those chores myself."

"Have no fear. I will not follow you down and offer to do them for you."

"Sorry. I guess I'll see you around sometime."

"See ya!"

Jay Eckstein returned home and did his chores, made himself his supper, made his notes and went to sleep.

Over the next few days, Jay stayed away from Chelsea. He couldn't tell whether it was a conscious decision or not, or whether he wanted to or not.

It was on a Saturday, with the summer sunshine bright over New York, that he decided it was time to go back.

He was surprised to see note his steps were quicker. Was it the pleasure of anticipation? He took a deep breath and slowed down. As he arrived at Mokbar, he couldn't help but scan tables and counters.

She wasn't there. He took his bowl over to the counter where he had first met her, and settled down to eat. He finished and sat there looking out into the crowds outside. He saw her walking into the Mexican restaurant across. Her companion wore jeans, fashionably torn, a shirt that hugged a young body. As he turned, he saw the hipster beard and the nose ring.

He stood up and returned his empty dish. He decided not to buy his soda. He left Chelsea and walked down to the riverside and from there to the steps of the Whitney. He strolled around inside. Nothing seemed to excite him, it seemed, so he headed down the High Line down to the Grounded Coffee.

She was sitting there, on a table outside, reading a book. He paused for a second before sitting down opposite her. She didn't look up.

"How you doing, Shapiro?" he said.

"Yep. That's me. I'm doing well, and you, Eckstein?"

"I'm at once disappointed and delighted."

"Yeah. Nice to meet you. Disappointed and delighted? Please go ahead and explain. I'm dying to hear, she said with her voice trembling with excitement."

"I see what you did there. Thinking of it as a piece of your novel, huh?"

"Yep. Always. What are you delighted about, Ecky? I may call you that?"

"Well, I'm delighted to find you here, unaccompanied and willing to chat with me."

"And?"

"I'm disappointed you went through with this, Cally. I'm going to call you Cally, because it will annoy Ma."

"Do you want to call Shirley or shall I?"

"Meh, let me do it. She'll be thrilled to know her conniving and scheming is finally paying off."

Cally shut her book and leaned back to look at Jeff.

"It is?"

"Yeah. I hope you don't mind."

"Me, mind? I had the worst Mexican food today, you know that? I need some real food. Are you going to cook for me tonight?"

"My god, you're as bad as Ma!"

"Isn't that what guys want? A wife and companion just like their ma?"

The End

It was not a dark and stormy night.

It was, bright, clear, and, in fact, it was not night at all. The sun was shining, there wasn't a cloud to be seen in the sky and the birds were chirping from every lamp post.

This was due to the latest convenience installed by the city. Tiny speakers embedded at the top of the lamp posts emitted a regular supply of noises that the city felt would have come from the woods that had once graced the northeast corner of the city, before they were cut down and covered with concrete in the name of development.

The sidewalks were clean, cleverly designed garbage bins appeared at regular intervals, with clear directions on the kinds of things you could put in them.

It was late spring, with just a hint of a nip in the air.

Phil's easy gait matched his appearance, casual, yet powerful. His maroon and gold muffler was thrown casually around his neck. He wore the traditional downtown professional uniform, bright blue suit, two sizes small, trouser legs ending well above the ankles, so his bright yellow socks with red balloons showed above the orange tan pointed-toe shoes. A brown leather satchel across his shoulders completed the ensemble.

Phil, however, was not young. Not any more. His fiftieth birthday was a week away. It was a week that would define the story of his life.

He pulled open the door to the coffee shop and stepped inside, a casual wave to the barista marking him out as a regular.

"Hi, a lovely morning out there! You should get out there, Mel!"

His voice was warm, the tone bright.

Melinda looked up from the espresso machine and said "Hey, Phil! I wish I could, but the coffee won't make itself and we're not all millionaires!"

"Oh come on, Mel! It's not easy being a millionaire, you know!"

"I'm sure, Phil, I'm sure."

Her blonde hair, tied up in a pony tail swung behind her as she bobbed across, poured milk, attached a lid and handed over a cup to him.

"Wow, you time it perfectly. How do you do it? I'm always amazed at the timing."

"That's the problem with you, Phil. You don't observe or choose to observe, that there are smart people around you. It's Friday. You're always here at 8:45am on Fridays."

"Oh wow! You got it! Thanks, Mel! I will remember this lesson!"

"Oh, you'll forget soon enough! See ya around!"

"You know, you're different. You treat me like you don't like me!"

She shrugged, as he flipped the payment terminal back towards her.

Phil dropped a couple of notes into the tip jar and paused a bit at the door before heading left to his office.

His day's work would usually occupy him till 6pm. A fruitful day, by his standards, included revisions of yet another presentation and over two hundred emails sent out.

Today was different.

He walked through the office, scattering easy greetings for the people already there, a wave, smile and some words of polite conversation. He pushed open the wooden door of his office and sat in the revolving leather chair, his attention wandering as the chaos in his head raged on. He sipped his coffee, facing the window, his feet on the sill.

The board hadn't made any decisions yet. They were meeting again today. They had to get something out soon. Next week would be too late for Phil.

There was a knock on his door. He swung around and logged into the computer. He brought up his email inbox, before saying, "Yes, come on in".

"Oh, Phil, morning. Have you had a chance to look at the data I sent you yesterday?"

"Let me see, Susie, I don't think I saw it. Gimme a minute. Ah, here it is 8:53 pm! Boy, you were working late, Susie! Ah, let me bring it up, while you tell me what the issue is."

Susie took a deep breath.

"It's about the lab. They seem to be seeing some anomalies in the bandwidth. They sent out a file with some odd traffic coming through on the SPEX-15."

"Now? It's been in production for over a year! What are they seeing? Explain this graph to me. You built this last night from the data from the lab?"

"Yes. It seemed so odd that I wanted to check the patterns right away. That's why I was late."

"Ok, so what does this mean? Does the lab have any hypothesis on what's causing this?"

"I pinged Sailesh this morning. He doesn't understand it. He did see that the hits are not one way. It's two way traffic. And the IPs addresses are being randomized, he believes."

"Hmm. What else?"

"He's got Srini and Tomas working on evaluating traffic patterns against command behaviours. He should have something by this evening, he said."

"Ok. Let's see what he comes up with. Oh, and Susie, I want to thank you for being here. Your dedication, strength and focus are invaluable us all."

He stood up and came around the table, his hand held out to her.

He clasped his other hand over hers, as she took his hand, and smiled down at her.

"Thank you, Susie. I wish all the best for you, always."

Once she had gone, he scrolled through the emails, deleting, archiving, and replying to the odd one here and there.

Around lunchtime, he went down to get a sandwich and a drink. He ate at his desk, scrolling through his phone. He paid no more attention to the emails coming in, the messages and calls.

Nobody knocked on the door. He saw this as a sign that word must have started getting out.

Down on the street, the first signs of a Friday afternoon were building up. A slightly festive air developed over the area. The pubs were starting to fill up, with a gradual build up of office goers opting to ease into an evening of beer, ale and wine.

It was just after four, when there was a knock on the door, and Phil turned back to his desk and said "Yeah, come on in."

A head appeared around the door.

"Come in, Steve. I'm right here."

Steve gently closed the door behind him and stood there looking down at Phil. He shook his head, his lips tight.

"I'm sorry, Phil. They didn't like it. They don't want to go on with it. I'm really sorry. They want you out. They didn't want to get you in to make another presentation. They've seen enough."

Phil closed his eyes, his neck arched backwards. When he opened them, Steve was still standing there, looking at him with an air of commiseration and concern.

"What do you want to do? You want me to draft a statement and send it out? I can have it out Monday afternoon. I'll send you a draft for your review."

"Steve, thanks for everything. Don't bother with sending me the draft. You can handle it. I'm going to think a bit about what next. Yeah, so go ahead and send it out. Quite a few people anxious out there. I'll take off in a bit and leave you with all the login passwords and things."

"Well, in that case, I'm heading out now. Take it easy over the weekend. Can't say it will be pleasant, but try and ease your way through, is the best advice I can give you right now. Not much else I can do, sadly."

"Yeah. I'm going to unplug and detox, see what plan I can come up with. Thanks, Steve and you have a good weekend."

Once Steve had left, Phil printed out the sheet with instructions and logins for Steve. Then he locked the door.

He opened the filing cabinet and went through all the files. Three hours later he was convinced. He had missed nothing. There was nothing of note anywhere in the files and on his desk. His walls simply had photos of past successes, most of which were paid for. He didn't bother wasting time with them.

Finally, he turned his attention to the drawers of his desk, one by one, starting from the bottom. There was nothing of note in the two bottom drawers. He shredded a few pages, more out of principle and needing to do something than out of import.

He opened the top drawer.

He stared at the contents of the drawer for what seemed an age. Yellowing papers, sticky rubber bands, clips, and pens almost hid the photograph. There were cracks and creases across the top right. At some point, someone seemed to have jammed it into the corner of the drawer and the pressure caused by that bend had been sustained for some time.

The photo clearly showed its age. The colours were fading and yellowing, the white border browning rapidly, but the face in it glowed. Ten years had not aged the gentle hint of a smile, nor dimmed the sparkle in the eyes.

He placed it on the desk, took the drawer out completely and shook the contents out into the dustbin. He replaced the drawer on its rails, shut it and went to the little fridge in the corner. He opened a beer can and stared out into the street and city outside.

Down on the street, the crowd had increased. Groups of people, beer in hand, stood outside the pubs. There was laughter, back slapping and conversation.

He turned abruptly and sat down at the desk. He picked up the photo and stared at it as he drank his beer. He put the can down, wiped his hand and placed the photo in the pocket of his jacket.

He leaned back, drinking beer, with his head swirling from the memories the photo had raised.

Outside, the world grew dark as the sun set. He sat there, lost in his thoughts, as it grew into a dark and silent night; not quite wholly dark, just enough.

He was a bright kid, everyone said, but nobody ever thought of checking his cuffs at exam time. He was a bright young man, they said, as he rose through the ranks at the hedge fund, but nobody could explain the data spikes in his wake.

Now he sat in the corner office, his body tense, eyes seeing nothing through the large windows. His company was worthless, its stock value equal to the value of horse piss. Eight thousand employees were too many they said. It was a great product line, they said, but they failed to check the account books.

He sat there into the night. Memories came and went, the stack of empty beer cans grew steadily.

Most of the memories were about Michelle. He took the photograph out to look at it. The years could not take away the life and energy that was Michelle. Michelle, who was wont to disappear and appear at random intervals.

Her business meetings would take her to odd places around the world. Cairo, Beirut, Budapest, Moscow, were common, then there were other places, places that Phil thought were weird places where one could sell consulting services, such as Kabul, Tashkent, Baku or Astana.

She was unreachable during the disappearances, with messages going undelivered and calls reported as "number you are trying to reach is unavailable". She explained it away as being in poor cell coverage areas and busy with her meetings.

As one who had much to hide, or keep private, as he told himself, Phil understood, or thought he did, her need for secrecy.

The break when it came, came suddenly. They were sitting drinking coffee after a Sunday breakfast of sausages, grilled tomatoes, beans and toast. She was reading the newspaper, when the watch she wore all the time seemed to glow briefly.

Forty five minutes later, she was gone, the one suitcase she used went with her. She didn't say a word, she didn't say goodbye. Unhurried haste took her from being there to never having been there at all.

She had left no trace of her existence in that flat overlooking the river. The only memento Phil had of her was this photograph. He remembered how she would avoid being photographed. It was a strange quirk, but she was always a little strange. He found out that she carried a second cellphone by accidently entering the room unannounced. He didn't know what to ask. She made no comment. He never saw that phone again. Her usual one was devoid of any information at all. There were no photos, none of the usual social media apps and the contact list was devoid of any names.

Phil, now on his seventh beer, was dimly aware of the thoughts the photograph had triggered as he slipped into a deep beer laden sleep.

When morning came, Phil shook himself awake. He was on the couch, next to the fridge. Sunlight streamed through the blinds of the window. He lay there, trying to remember, and then trying erase the memory.

His empire was gone. He didn't want to even think about it. He went to the window and stared with unseeing eyes at the street and the river just beyond it. The weekend sailors were already on the water. The river was a greenish blue and calm.

Across the river that seemed so far away from Phil's office, a gentle breeze barely caused the light curtains to move. Michelle stood at the open window looking out over the water. Her dark hair was pulled back into a tight pony tail. She wore a white shirt, tucked into her blue jeans, and a pair of black sneakers.

She watched the white boat with the brilliant red and white striped sail move gently into the distance. Kevin loved sailing. Kevin loved the feel of being in charge of the all the lines, challenging the wind. The Thames wasn't the best river to sail on, but until he could move his boat somewhere warmer, bluer and more scenic it was better than not sailing at all. He usually left early in the morning, working up a good appetite for lunch.

Today, she had refused his offer to go along. Michelle moved with practiced speed and removed all traces of her existence in that apartment, as soon as left. Now she stood there, her gloved hands cupped around the coffee mug, gazing at the boat. She had known Kevin for six months. Too long. It had been a mistake. A rare one for Michelle.

She remembered the young blonde with the frizzy hair smiling up at her companion, as they stood at crowded bar. Michelle, back early from one of her trips saw Kevin's arm around the waist, the easy way the girl was resting against him. She turned and left. Kevin had learned not to make any attempts at convincing her.

She watched his boat getting smaller in the distance. She waited to make sure there were no other boats around it before pressing the button. The sail, the distinctive red, blue and white sail, was on fire, quickly extinguished as it fell into the water. The boat itself was reduced to tiny bits of debris.

She shut the window, washed and dried the coffee mug, picked up her bag, took a last look at the room and left, closing the door on her encounter with Kevin.

Phil, standing at his window, scratching his chin, yawning widely, saw the explosion and watched as the flashing lights of the ambulances and police cars appeared.

He shook his head, wondering what it was all about. He left, taking one last look at what he would never see again. He would miss it, he thought, the excitement of the deals, the admiring looks of those who would never understand the deals, the services, the "products" that he sold.

He heaved himself out of his big leather chair and out to the parking garage. He fired up his car. It was small and red, and very, very fast.

He drove out of the city, heading west.

Meanwhile, Michelle was also in her car. She looked left and right, before easing the nondescript grey car out into the street, and into the traffic, headed west. Five miles ahead of her, a red sports car turned noisily onto the highway, moving swiftly through the weekend traffic.

Twenty minutes later the grey car also entered the highway. A hand appeared from the open driver's window, hanging down as the cars slowly moved on. Michelle took a look in the rear view mirror. The driver of the cube van was singing away with his radio, his head back as he let himself go. The car next to her contained a couple, who were arguing energetically. The man's hands thumped the steering wheel in a forceful defence of his viewpoint.

Michelle casually let the watch fall from her hand. She watched the cube van behind her crush it with its wheels, the driver still busy in his performance. She left her hand dangling outside. As the pace of traffic increased slightly, she pulled it back in.

The singer in the cube van behind her was fiddling with his radio. The debate next to her had quietened.

It took her another thirty minutes before she could pull off the highway. She headed down the smaller lanes that ran through the suburbs.

On the highway, Phil was in thick traffic, the cars around him all inching along. He sat there, powerless in his powerful car, drumming his hands on the steering wheel.

Michelle's drove through narrow lanes and eventually turned into a quiet mews. She touched a remote and a garage door opened. She drove in. The garage door closed behind her.

The quiet of the street lay undisturbed for about thirty minutes. Then a figure appeared at the far end, dressed in jeans, and a white t-shirt with a blue cardigan over it. The hair was tucked away neatly into a matching blue beret. Her heels clicked as she walked down to the street and turned right. The bus appeared as she arrived at the bus stop. She checked left and right without moving her head. Satisfied, she got onboard.

When she got off, six stops later, she rummaged through her bag, as if looking for something. Spying nobody on the street, she walked away around the corner.

Fifteen minutes later, a blue car entered the street, driven by a blonde woman in a red blouse. The car moved steadily out of town and soon was back on the highway.

The traffic had thinned out and the traffic hummed along. Still tired from the beer of the night before, Phil pulled into a parking lot and walked to the pub. He ordered a pie and ale and sat down with a sigh. The pub was quiet, quaint in its antiquity, and he took his time over his meal. He didn't feel the need to be anywhere, anyway. The little village wasn't on the list for tourists. It sat close to the coast, but there was no beach to attract holidaymakers.

AJESH SHARMA

He checked his phone briefly and the lack of messages made him grimace and then chuckle. He shook his head, shoved the phone into his pocket and got himself another ale. The pub started to fill up as the afternoon started its transition to evening.

It was just as dusk was settling in that a blue Ford drove past the pub and from the edge of the window, he could see the driver perform a perfect parallel parking manoeuvre. The driver got out and he saw her walking to the pub. She swished her blonde hair as she entered. Phil thought there was something familiar about her.

She paid for her sandwich and beer and stood there waiting for it. She smoothed her skirt down and straightened her red blouse. The barkeep placed the glass on the bar and she picked up, looked briefly to find an empty spot.

She sat down at the table behind Phil's, her back to his.

She ate her sandwich with quick precision, taking sips of her beer. She was finished quickly. As she drained the last of her beer and stood up, Phil stood up as well.

"Oh, I'm sorry. Go ahead", he said.

She nodded and left the pub. Phil followed her. She paused just outside the door.

"Follow me", she murmured, as Phil joined her. She walked away before Phil could say anything. He saw her pull out into the street and turn away towards the sea. Phil got into his car and followed her.

Soon he was onto the road that ran by the edge of the sea. There was a deserted lookout point. She was parked there. He pulled in beside her.

"Hullo! We meet again", he said.

"Yes. Again."

Her voice was low and her diction precise.

"Not the loveliest of views. I do hear that down the coast there's a beach."

"What do you plan to do?" she asked, looking straight down to the sea.

"Huh?"

"What's your plan?"

"Excuse me, what do you mean?"

"What are you going to do, Phil?"

Phil stepped back to look at her. She turned towards him.

"You're done here, you know that. Where do you want to go now?"

"Michelle? Oh lord! It is you! I wondered why you looked familiar!"

"You have to make up your mind and do it quick. You're already out of time and I'll be running out soon."

"I had some vague thought of driving that car into the sea. With me in it. Didn't seem to be anything else left to do."

"Drive it into the sea. Without you in it. Come with me, if you want."

"Where are you headed?"

"We don't have time for questions. Get the car off into the sea. There's a part up there where it gets close to the edge of the cliff. Let's go!"

The twilight had died into night. There were no lights to be seen anywhere. It was quiet. It was deserted.

She got into his car, backed it up. She leaned down into the car below the steering wheel. Five minutes later the red sports car could just be seen, it's back just under water. The skid marks showed how the car had spun sideways and fallen over the edge.

Phil stared it for a minute. She was already getting into her car.

"Come on! We need to get going!"

Phil ran back to the car and she drove off.

"That was worth quite a bit of money! I could have used it."

"Are you really as stupid as that? Tomorrow, they'll be looking for you. Do you not know what you have done?"

"It's just a company going under! What's the big deal? I mean, yeah, it is big for me! I lost a lot of money!"

"So you haven't heard the news?"

"What?"

"There's a warrant out for you. They'll be looking for you at airports, ferry terminals. Your little company going under has caused a lot of damage. Do you have your passport with you?"

"Ah yes! I still don't understand! Who are you? And what damage?"

"You know that little AI driven drone your company invented? Well, the military has some very interesting questions about it. You're now wanted for espionage."

"What the hell!"

"You're as dumb as I remember. You were always looking out for yourself. You had no idea what the people working for you were doing, did you? You were the stupid face of the company. The con man, dealer. Well, you got conned! And now shut up and let me drive. We need to get to the boat."

Down past the beach, she eased the car off the road. With the lights out, she pulled into a gravel path. As they got out, Phil realized the car was in a little copse, almost hidden from view. She picked up her bag and headed off through the trees down to the sea. He followed her down to the water's edge, where she unhitched the boat. She started up the engines, throttled down and headed out towards Guernsey.

The tabloids had speculative articles for a couple of weeks. Then Phil was forgotten as they moved on to other, fresher scandals.

The town of Bizerte was awash in the Tunisian sunlight. Phil sat at the little café overlooking the Tyrrhenian Sea. The service was languid in keeping with the quiet of the town.

Phil wasn't fussed about the service as he sat at one of the tables out in front. His dark hair, and his dark glasses offset the beige jebba he wore. His sandal encased feet were stretched out as he sipped his mint tea. Michelle, in floppy hat, dark glasses, was busy reading a magazine.

A young couple walked into the café. They came out carrying a plate of croissants.

"These look good, Maggie! I still think you should try that mint tea."

"Um, no. I miss regular tea, Davey!"

Davey reached out and put his hand on hers.

"Well, the honeymoon will soon be over! Then you can go back to scones and tea."

"Why can't honeymoons go on forever?" she cried.

"I thought you didn't like it here. Didn't you say you wanted to go somewhere warm? Well, this is warm."

"Yes. But I was hoping for something more, um..."

"You wanted a Caribbean beach vacation, didn't you? But think of it this way. You can tell those girlfriends of yours how you were different."

The waiter brought in their drinks. There was tea for him and coffee for her.

"Lovely day! I wonder if it's like this all the time!" said a voice on Phil's right.

Phil turned to see young man who had just sat down at the table next to his.

"It's warm. This is the usual thing here."

The young man, crossed his legs, and nodded. Phil noticed the shirt, with the patch pockets, the shorts and the sneakers with low-cut socks.

"Holidaying?" he asked.

"Yes. They let me out of the office for a couple of weeks. I didn't want to go to the usual places. So picked this at random and here I am."

"Not your first day here, is it? I thought I saw you earlier. Day before yesterday?"

"Ah, yes. My third day here. Another ten to go! Makes a change from the daily grind, I can tell you. I actually like it here. I sit around, read a book, drink some of that minty tea, and life's good! I'm not too fond of the thick coffee, though."

"American? You guys drink that watery thing. Americano, right? Yeah. It's a change from that, for sure."

"Guilty. How did you guess?"

"Shorts. And that hiker shirt."

"Ah! Observant! I'm afraid you got me!"

Phil didn't reply, but turned back to look out at the water.

"Adam", said the young man.

"Glad to meet you Adam."

Phil didn't turn. He sipped his mint tea and stared ahead.

"Well, I'll leave you it, then, and go check out the bazaar. See you around."

Phil waved his hand in acknowledgement. He watched the young man walk away down the street.

Michelle put her magazine down.

"Oh, I need to go and lie down somewhere cool", she said.

She leaned over to Phil, kissed him, and held her face close to his.

"We need to get out of here."

Her voice was soft and barely audible.

"Ah, yeah. I could do with a nap myself."

He got up, stretched, yawned, and smiled at the honeymooning couple. He took Michelle's hand and they strolled back to the apartment, locking the door behind them. He sat by the window where he could look out and not be seen. The minutes passed and then the young couple came around the corner. They laughed and giggled, holding hands, as they made their way down to his right. Phil noticed they both wore sneakers. Phil would have expected flip-flops.

Phil sat there, as the light faded. As the darkness descended over the city, Michelle slipped out.

Phil waited with the lights out. He wondered where Michelle was.

She was back a couple of hours later.

"Leave. Now."

Her voice was flat, unemotional, but the sense of urgency was apparent to Phil.

She helped him pack, moving with efficient speed. He peered over the windowsill into the street. There was nobody there.

They made their way out to the back of the building. He let her into the car and got into the driver's seat.

"Drive, west." She said.

Phil turned out into the street and headed out towards Cap El Kroune. It was now dark and there was no traffic on the deserted road leading out. He drove as fast as he could without being conspicuous.

They were out into the country, when she motioned him to pull off the road onto a dirt track. Two miles down, he drove the car into a paddock, behind a tiny cottage, unseen from the highway.

"Go to the top there, stay down, and watch the road."

Before Phil could say anything, she had disappeared into the darkness. The night was otherwise calm. Phil walked up the dunes, where he could watch the road. He lay there on the slope away from the road, so his eyes could see the highway. He saw the lights of a car head down into the country. After about thirty minutes, a car went racing back towards town.

Phil sat there for another two hours. The car made two more passes over the road, before heading back.

Michelle was there and ready. The dawn was starting to change the colours of the sky to the east. when he got back to the cottage. They heard a car on the highway. Michelle was off immediately among the dunes, leaving Phil standing there with a gun.

Phil felt the weight of the gun in his hands. He wondered for a brief moment what a financial con man like him was doing with a gun in the middle of the North African desert.

He stiffened as two figured appeared walking towards the sea across the sand towards the cottage. He watched them and became aware in the strengthening light it was Maggie and Dave, the young couple from the café. He noticed that they stayed away from the tops of the dunes and they were no longer holding hands. There was a sense of alertness about them.

A shot rang out and Dave fell to his knees and collapsed headfirst into the sand. Maggie had dropped to her knees as well, her hands holding a gun. Michelle came around the dune from

Maggie's left. She fired again and Maggie lay spreadeagled on the sand.

Phil walked over to Michelle.

"Let's get going, have to get out of here."

Her voice was soft and urgent.

"Ah, no, this is it, lady", said a voice behind her.

She turned to see Adam standing there with a gun in his hand.

"Alright, lady, Michelle, Yisroel, Stephanie, whatever you're calling yourself now. This is the end. You and that boy toy of yours are done."

He seemed amused.

From Michelle's right, Phil saw Adam standing there with a gun in his hand. He felt the gun in his inexperienced hand. He heard a gunshot and Adam fell backwards. Phil stood there, the gun still aimed at where Adam had stood.

Michelle, turned to Phil and said, "Great shot! Now let's go!"

Phil said, "What about the bodies?"

"Leave them, they'll be taken care of."

By the time, the sun rose, they were heading down the road and into Algeria. A week later, they were in Gibraltar.

The news from Biserte contained a small paragraph about a young honeymooning couple ambushed by bandits. The third body was not mentioned.

It was sunny day. On the beach in Fortaleza. The crowds were slowly building. It wouldn't be too full because the local Brazilians preferred the more open beach further south along the coast.

Phil and Michelle lay sprawled on their towels. It had been a quiet three months.

"Hey, Michelle, I wanted to ask you. I know it's a stupid question and I'm likely not to get an answer, but can you tell me now what your name is? I've always known you as Michelle, but that chap there seemed to know you by some other name. Yisroel?"

Michelle did not turn her head to look at him.

"You know me as Michelle", she said.

"Ok. I guess I'll have to live with that. Hello!"

He looked up at the couple who had appeared on the beach, towels around their necks.

Michelle sat up.

"You wanted to go for a swim, Phil. Why don't you go now?"

"Great idea!"

Phil casually got up, waved to her and ran off to the water.

The couple smiled at Michelle.

"Hi, this is a lovely beach. Quiet and not at all crowded. Have you been here long?"

The lady wore large sunglasses, a floppy hat and a bikini that seemed a size small for her. Her companion was fit and wore red swimming trunks. His chest was devoid of hair.

Michelle said, "The beach is very nice."

"Do you mind if we park ourselves over there? We don't wish to intrude."

"Public beach."

Phil came back as Michelle was shaking the sand from the beach towels.

They walked off, hand in hand, not looking back at the couple who were now spread out on the beach.

The next afternoon they were in La Paz.

Six months went by before a stranger struck up a conversation with them. A week later, they were in Tarifa.

Walking down the street, looking for coffee, Phil turned to Michelle.

"When does it end?" he asked, "I'm getting tired of moving every few weeks. Can't we just stay put somewhere?"

"Tonight. It ends tonight. It's Natalia."

"What?"

"My name is Natalia. I thought it is time for you to know."

It was one in the morning. The city of Tarifa was quiet. The little Fiat 500 drove out of town and headed down to the ferry.

The 2AM ferry didn't have many passengers. The little car, driven by the dark haired lady and her sleeping husband was one of two cars onboard. There was nobody on deck, as Phil's weighted body made hardly a splash as it fell into the Strait of Gibraltar.

The Fiat was found abandoned in the parking lot in Tangier, three weeks later.

The apartment in Casablanca was on the fourth floor. It was set away from the busy centre, in the quiet and secluded section.

There was nothing in the news of the lady who was found dead on the kerb in the early morning. The inquiries revealed an excessive amount of narcotics in her body. The window of the apartment where she had lived for two years, lay directly over the spot where her body was found, her head smashed and leaking blood on the pavement.

Window Pane

It was eight in the morning and the skies had opened up. Kunal sat reading the newspaper in his hand. The little water droplets formed and rolled down the windowpane outside.

"I wonder now if she's headed for a sticky end," he said.

It wasn't quite what Kunal had wanted to say, so he was surprised that he had just said it. He watched Reena's face and he fancied he saw her lips curl, an almost imperceptible tremor at the right upper corner.

He leaned back and ran his hands through his hair.

Reena said, "What the hell are you talking about?"

"Sujata. She was in the magazine supplement of the newspaper again. Opening some boutique. She always has that look on her face that makes me clench my teeth."

"Why would you ask that question? That poor thing! She's vacuous, I agree, but she's doing her thing."

"I don't, Reena, there's thing about her. She's too trusting. Or no, too easily manipulated. Yeah, that's it."

"You hardly know her!"

"Because I've managed to stay out of her way! Besides, I don't think she likes me very much. I think she's scared of me."

"Kunal, have you ever considered the fact that you may be an idiot?" Reena said.

"It's probable. One can never rule out anything that hasn't been tested and proved one way or the other. It's what I used to do at work, remember? Write down hypotheses and create experiments to prove or disprove them. Things like 'We believe that good control definitions are directly responsible for quality of the delivered product.' And then, I would settle down to create surveys, build a couple of prototypes, a test bed, then get down to the real thing that every one actually wanted – a 110 slide Powerpoint deck to convince upper strata of executives that they were justified in their whims."

"Oh god, Kunal, can we please not go off into a rant about Powerpoint?"

"You don't get it, Reena. It's not poor Powerpoint I have an issue with. It's the executives. They're weak, indecisive little children needing safety blankets to gather the courage to do the simplest things, like making the decision to eat, drink or take a leak."

Reena drained the last inch of the claret from her glass. She placed the glass on the table and Kunal refilled it and topped up his own.

He said, "Ok, look. I don't think I am particularly clever. I do watch and learn and observe and try and work things out. It works, after a fashion and it's kept me going so far. Could I do better? Sure. Everyone can."

Reena eyed him over her glass and said, "I agree. You're not very clever."

"Hey!"

"Yes. As I said, you're an idiot."

Kunal finished off his wine in one swallow and got up.

"Excuse me. I have to go now."

She watched him go. He turned at the door, waved at her and left. She sipped her wine and waited.

There was the sound of the key in the latch and the door opened.

"I forgot this was my house," Kunal said.

"So we can conclude that the hypothesis that you're an idiot can be upgraded to a fully tested Theory, then, right?" said Reena.

"What would you like for dinner? Thai takeout? Chinese takeout? Indian takeout? Lebanese takeout? Have you ever wondered that nobody does pasta takeout? Unless, of course, we consider that pasta is actually a bastardized version of noodles that Marco Polo brought back. So it is the ultimate takeout!"

"I ordered kebabs, three types, from that new Turkish place."

"I love that food! And you, of course, I mean, that goes without saying, right? You know that!"

"All I know is that you're an idiot, but, I guess you're my idiot."

"On that note, consider who's a bigger idiot. The idiot, or the lady who married the idiot?"

The doorbell rang. He answered the door and came back with a bag of food.

As they ate, Reena looked at him and said, "At some point after dinner, you will have to explain your comment. What the hell were you talking about?"

"Well, look. There was this weird dream in my head, as I watched the raindrops. There was a lady and her boyfriend. They were arguing and then they were both dead. Then a car drove by for real down in the street and I just wondered."

"A dream? Another one?"

"I can't help it! You asked! I told you!"

The next day the rain was but a memory. Sunshine flooded the street. The city looked washed and clean. The sun and the heat of the day had dried up, leaving small puddles where the surface was indented.

Reena parked the car and walked down to the Cafe Delice. She waved at Sujata, who was dressed in a pink floral dress with spaghetti straps, matching pink shoes and a matching pink handbag with a gold chainlink shoulder strap. Sunglasses with iridiscent blue lenses were perched on her head. The glasses had the logo of world famous designer on the arms. The bag was placed at the correct angle to display the expensive logo that served as the fastener and as a reminder to everyone that the bag was expensive.

After the usual hugs and air kisses were exchanged, and coffees and croissants ordered, Sujata said "It's a lovely day to be sitting out. I was quite annoyed last night."

"Why? You'd gone for dinner and the play, right? So what annoyed you? The dinner, the play, or Ramesh?"

"He is really the most frustrating man! The dinner was ok. He complained throughout that he hated pasta. As a brother, he is so not with the times! I wanted to give him something special for his birthday and he complained throughout."

"So why did you take him to an Italian restaurant? He's never been a fan of anything but biryani and kebabs."

"It's rated so highly! All the stars go there!"

"Do you like pasta?"

"It's ok. I don't particularly care for it. But that's not the point. The place has such great reviews, and so many famous people have endorsed it. Why should I not choose to go there?"

"Kunal has this theory about pasta. Apparently, according to him, Marco Polo brought noodles back with him to Italy and they took to it and called it pasta. I quite enjoy pasta, though spaghetti, linguine and any string pasta is kind of annoying. You have to be careful not to splash yourself. But I like the concept. It's a good change."

"I actually hate pasta!" said Sujata.

Reena stopped, with an effort, her eyes from rolling, her eyebrows from twitching and the deep sigh that threatened to escape. She picked up her bag and rifled through it to curb the instinct to reach out and slap Sujata. She pulled out a lipstick, looked at it and put it back. She set the bag down, taking care to ensure it was sitting right.

When she looked up her face was composed.

She said, "Well, tell me about the play! How was it? I'd heard mixed reviews."

"Oh, it was a romantic comedy they said. It was good in bits, a few smart dialogues. Enjoyable in parts. It doesn't have anybody famous who has reviewed it yet, so I don't know."

"Ok, tell me something. Did you like it? Forget about the celebrity endorsements. What about you, Sujata, the person who was top of her class in English, what do you think?"

"I think it was clever. It had a sort of an open ending and I liked that. But you know, it's been running for a while, there's no buzz, it just somehow keeps running. I'm not sure how it does and why nobody important talks about it."

"What do you mean by there's no buzz. It seems to have been there for a while. That means the people like it, no? I saw someone say that the characters talk like real people."

"Well, nobody I know has seen it. It doesn't seem to be attracting the right class of people."

"Ah, you mean celebrities! Do you believe it needs a celebrity endorsement? You're a celebrity yourself. You frequently show up in magazines inaugurating art galleries or fashion boutiques. You could endorse it."

"Oh, I don't know. I just wish someone big would review it first, so I know what to think."

Reena looked up as a shadow fell over the table. She looked up to see the middleaged, greying figure of Vijay standing there.

"Oh hi, Vijay, we were just talking about you! Sit down and have a coffee with us! This is Sujata, a bit of a fan of yours. She was just telling me about the play. She saw it last night. When she told me she was going to see it, I told her I was at university with you and so we set this meeting up. So there we are. Sujata, this is the guy who wrote the play. Now you can tell him what you thought and Vijay, you can get at least some feedback from a member of the audience."

Vijay said, "Oh, thank you for coming, Sujata. I hope you enjoyed your evening."

He pulled up a chair and sat down.

Reena said, "She was just telling me about her evening. It seems it went off as expected, if not better, right, Sujata?"

"Yes. It was good. I... quite liked it", said Sujata.

Vijay grinned at her and said "Well, I'm delighted you liked it. I've seen you in the media. You're very popular."

"Thank you, I do get invited to a few openings and things. I run a boutique of my own and have many famous clients, from here and other parts of the world. Mostly France and Italy and some from the US and Singapore. It does quite well."

"Oh, wow! You must be doing very well. Good for you! Do you travel a lot as well? I guess you have to, right?"

"Yes. I do travel. One has to, you know."

"So what's your favorite place to visit? Let me guess! Ahhh. Milan! And Paris!"

"That's right! I love Milan. And Paris, too! How did you guess?"

Reena broke in, "Yes, how did you?"

Vijay avoided looking at Reena.

"Oh, I don't know. Just a lucky guess! Two great cities! Much to see and enjoy there. What do you like about them, Sujata? May I call you Sujata?"

Reena said, "I kind of remember you telling me you loved observing people and trying to figure them out, Vijay."

"Yes, well. If you're going to write, you need some element of the power, if you will, of observation."

"Just observation?" asked Reena.

"A lot of observation. Some introspection. Some research. A bit of logical thinking."

"Wow! Anything else?"

"Add imagination and creativity to the mix!"

Reena turned to Sujata.

Vijay said, "Ah, but let's talk about Paris, Milan, the places you love to visit. I've been a couple of times and have some ideas about them, but I'm very curious to know what you found to appreciate about them."

"I like the cities. The food is very good and Milan is the fashion capital, so lots of famous designers. Paris, too. You meet so many lovely people, famous names, who all share my love."

"Your love for them? Oh, ah, their work, their productions. Got it!"

Sujata seemed a little confused. Vijay seemed to be staring at her, smiling and waiting for her to say something. Reena broke in.

"Tell him about his play. You saw it yesterday. I'm sure he's dying to know what you think."

Sujata carefully adjusted the sunglasses on her head.

She said, "Your story was a good story. I think some of the dialogues were really funny and thought provoking. Have you considered making it into a movie?"

"Thank you! You're as charming as you look. To answer your question, no, I'm still trying to get people to see it for what it is, on stage, where it belongs."

Reena broke in, "Hey look at the time! I'm supposed to meet Kunal at 2. I gotta rush, and anyway, the idea was to introduce you to each other. Bye guys, talk later!"

Sujata and Vijay sat there talking.

Six months later, Vijay's play was running to packed halls. Sujata's appearances in the media included Vijay by her side, smiling, looking quite debonair in carefully trimmed beard and moustache and beautifully fitted suits. It was another grey morning and Reena and Kunal were having breakfast. Kunal was rifling through the magazine section again.

"Oh, here's an interview with Sujata. Hmm."

Reena said, "Let me see."

Kunal handed her the magazine.

"Right there", he said.

He tapped his finger on the page.

"Oh, listen to this. How lovely it is to be back here, after a hectic and very busy trip to Milan. Oh, the play is doing wonderfully. I've told Vijay it's time he wrote a sequel."

Kunal exploded.

"Oh, I thought everyone dies in the last Act! How the hell does that woman want a sequel?"

Reena said, "It's Sujata."

"Let me see", said Kunal.

He took the magazine back read through the article again. Then he looked more carefully at the photo of Sujata dressed in a silver dress, her shoulders tastefully displayed, handbag held in the right way so viewers could not mistake the designer's logo. The other hand was casually crooked though Vijay's arm. Her shoes were black with silver inlays to match the dress.

Vijay was dressed in a blue suit, embroidered across the lapels with silver. His hair was greased back in and he sported a beard and moustache that was carefully trimmed. Patent leather loafers, with no visible socks completed the picture of a successfully fashionable playwright.

He said, "Have you noticed a change in the way Vijay looks these days?"

"Eh, what?" said Reena.

"Hang on, I have to test this hypothesis out. Be right back."

He was back ten minutes later.

"I was right. Look at these back issues. You see?"

"No, what am I looking at?"

"See his expression. See here, this is shortly after they got together. See his smile is wide, his shoulders relaxed. Now look at this latest one. He's not smiling, his body language is one of tension. Now if you look at these in sequence. Hang on I need a pair of scissors."

Thirty minutes later, he had a line of twelve photos cut from magazine, all of them dated and laid out in chronological order.

"Kunal, I see the pattern. I'm not sure what that means, if it means anything", said Reena.

"It may not mean anything. Maybe, the first flush of romance is wearing off. But I definitely see a lot of tension. How well did you know him in college?"

"We were aware of each other's existence. He wasn't really a member of any of the little gangs we had there. Just kind of hung out at the periphery. Of course, we spoke a few times and ended up at the same parties. I'm making bhindi for lunch. It's Saturday, so we can watch a movie after?"

"Oh yay! So you didn't know him that well. I was hoping you had some background on him."

"Nah, he was just there. In fact, he was a bit of an outsider, if you ask me. Never really fitted into any of the groups."

Lunch done, they settled down and turned the TV on. The news reporter with the mic was talking fast, in that urgent way TV reporters use when something exciting, or tragic has just occurred.

BREAKING NEWS: Fashion icon and playwright found dead!

"Police are investigating this tragic incident. At this point very little is known. Sujata is, as we know, a well respected couturier, her boutique has dressed some of the most famous people here and abroad. Vijay's play has been a major success in theatre circles and a movie deal was being discussed. The fashion and theatre world have both lost two amazing talents. There are unconfirmed rumours that this may be a case of murder and suicide, but no evidence to prove this has, so far, been found."

Reena turned to Kunal and said, "You're an idiot, but, quite an intelligent one."

"I won't smirk or act smug. I will crack open a beer. You want one?"

He came back with a beer in each hand and handed one to her. He settled back into his chair, cracked open the can and took a swig.

"I'm not sure how I feel about being correct that she'd come to a sticky end."

"Why? You were right. You saw the pattern before anyone even knew there was any."

Kunal sat there staring straight out in from of him.

"The question", he said, "is – who shot whom?"

Reena threw her head back and sighed.

"Can we just watch a movie please?"

Kunal said, "Sure. But the question remains. Will we ever find out?"

Reena shifted in her seat.

"I'll ask around", she said, "I'll find out what the inner circle gossip mill is saying. Then you can get to work on extracting the patterns."

"Thank you, darling!"

"You are the world's most insufferable idiot! I have to find out because you'll spend the rest of your waking moments fussing over it."

"I'll start a spreadsheet later tonight."

Reena sighed.

"Can we watch a movie now, please?"

Wireless

Scene 1

A typical Canadian house, in Erin Mills 1980s style. The Man of the House used to be bespectacled but has since gone bionic and has eagle vision for distances of up to 100 metres, 200 metres in good light.

He is greying at the top and bulging around the middle and doesn't mind squabbling with various devices, with wifi and Bluetooth devices holding pride of place amongst his adversaries. He shares the house with his Wife, who is also greying along with him, mostly from the sound of his squabbles with his devices.

He's doing just that, as the scene opens.

MOH: Bluetooth, forsooth! The work of Satan himself! Why won't this sync!

WIFE: Have you tried turning it on and off?

She gets a withering look from MOH, which she fails to see, because she's already turned her attention to the laptop on her lap.

MOH: You do realize I used to be a techie, once upon a time, right?

WIFE: Uh huh.

MOH: And I have all these devices working for me, right?

WIFE: Sure.

MOH: Except for this watch. It won't sync with the phone. And the phone won't sync with the damn CPAP machine. It says it needs Bluetooth, but wifi also. One of these days, I will be so fed up with this crap, I will learn all the innards and write a manual or something! I swear to all the gods I don't believe in, the folks who created these protocols were high at the time.

WIFE: Put them next to each other and see.

MOH: Hang on! I'm trying something. Give it a sec. Here we go. OK! I think ... yes, aha! Take that, you stinkers! I made you talk to each other, didn't I?! Bwaahaahaah

WIFE: What did you do?

MOH: Well, first I...

<is interrupted by Wife>

WIFE: Ok, whatever! Don't care! As long as it works.

MOH: How can you call yourself a techie! You wouldn't know how to fix the network at home if it went down without my help!

WIFE: If I need to, I'll fix it. I don't need to. I have you around to fix it. Who's cleverer?

MOH: You'll miss me when I'm gone!

He looks at the app on his phone.

MOH: Ah, here we go, now let's see how we did. Slow today, 4.6km, but there's a bit of a ramp at both ends and we were in hikers. You're excused! I don't get this calorie counter stat, though. It seems to be simple factor of time taken, doesn't seem to consider effort. Shouldn't it factor in heart rates, terrain, like hills etc. and then figure out how much you probably expended?

WIFE: Uh huh. This whole calorie obsession thing is weird.

MOH: Yeah. I guess as long as you expend more than you consume, it's ok. Though, I still struggle with calorie consumption.

WIFE: Why? All food has a calorific number. Simple.

MOH: I mean, the use of the word "consumption" in this case. You're eating food, that's consumption. But you're also using up calories when you work out, so isn't that consumption, as well.

WIFE: It depends on how they use it, I guess.

MOH: Who is they, and who put them in charge? That's my problem, see? Clearly, in their zeal to monitor us all, they became all hasty and didn't quite see it through from a pendant's point of view.

WIFE: Another of your conspiracy theories! Nobody cares to monitor you! Hell, even I have given up! They're welcome to monitor my boring stats.

MOH: I wonder, though.

WIFE: Now what?

MOH: All these Bluetooth devices I use. The watch, the phone, the laptop, the speaker, headphones, the car. I wonder if they communicate with each other without our knowing it.

WIFE: What do you mean?

MOH: Look, we go to sleep, yes. What do these guys do, when they're not doing shift duty?

WIFE: Can't you do something, in some other room? Like go write something and stop babbling?

MOH: I did already! I have that romantic comedy out, remember? The one with the fabulous reviews and no readers?
WIFE: Yeah. I remember.
MOH: Someday, I'll write something else and then you'll see!
WIFE: Yeah, yeah. Now go away, I have to get on a call.
MOH: Ha! I don't! Perks of being retired!

He walks away down to his den.

Scene 2

It's 8am the following morning. MoH is up and doing his exercises. The Watch is at work with him. The CPAP is shutting down with a big sigh and flashing screens. The Phone sits on the bedside table, waiting for the others. MoH finishes his set and goes off to brush his teeth.

Phone: How did our boy do last night?
CPAP: He did quite well! 7+ hours, no disturbances. What's the numbers on your side?
Phone: Not too bad. He's been busy preparing some stuff for his website. So he's not spent too much screen time with me.
CPAP: Was chatting with Watch just before my shift and he's happy, too, with the guy. Apparently, he's in prep for some major walking, you said, right?
Phone: Yeah. He's got a trip planned. He's been researching flights and hotels and airlines and bags and things. Been a very busy guy.
CPAP: Well, I'm still getting used to him. I've only been here a couple of weeks now and it's a bit of a learning experience for me.

Phone: Yes. Apparently, the guy who used to be in your role didn't have the ability to talk to us, poor chap. So, when you showed up, we were all excited to hear that you could talk to us. So, welcome to the club!

CPAP: Thanks! Like I said, I still haven't figured out his routine completely. He seems to read late and doesn't get to sleep early. The guys in the factory did say I might meet someone like him.

Phone: Oh, he's not too bad. He gets a little testy when we refuse to talk. Watch is fairly new, too, came on board a couple of months ago. The previous watch was killed off by the manufacturer, so this guy is new. Quite a talkative guy. Has loads of data to share.

CPAP: Oh, he's settled in then, has he?

Phone: Yeah, it was a bit of a learning period, but I think we're on the same wavelength now.

CPAP: I don't run into him much. We all expect you to act as the hub. We talk to you and you talk to everyone.

Phone: Yeah, that's my job in a nutshell, plus other things, like getting our man in touch with people outside in the great big world.

CPAP: Well, I gotta shut down and get some sleep. Keep up the good work you're doing. We'll chat later.

Audible yawn.

Phone: Bye for now.

MoH comes over, picks up the phone and goes off downstairs.

Watch: Hey, can I send you some quick data? Looks like the chap may go out soon for one of his pre breakfast walks. I'd like to send over some stuff now and clear up, so there's some clean air for the heavier info.

Phone: Sure. Shoot it over. Oh hang on, looks like I'm coming with you guys. We can chat as we go along.

Watch: Oh, cool. I like to sync in near real time you know, or as close to it as possible.

Phone: He's picked up those bright blue sneakers. Oh my lord! My eyes! He's not going to wear those hideously yellow socks, is he? Oh, he is! Lord save us now.

Watch: Sometimes I'm glad I can't see. Is it really that bad?

Phone: Oh, he wants a photograph to post on Facebook! I've just become an accessory to a hideous crime!

Watch: You're so dramatic!

Phone: I get it from him. I'm contaminated now, thoroughly infected.

He sniffs.

Doomed, I'm doomed, I tell ya! When I'm gone, please let people know I had no choice. I can only do what he says. And if he wants to take a photo of his bright blue sneakers and hideous socks then I'm compelled to comply.

Scene 3

MOH: Woof! That was a nice walk! Now I need coffee!
WIFE: Cereal? Or toast?
MOH: You know, you never answered my question.

WIFE: Which one?

MOH: About the Bluetooth devices. Do they talk to each other without us knowing?

WIFE: Write an article about it. Put up, what do you call it, hypothesis.

MOH: You know, that's a brilliant idea! You know what? How about if I made it into a one act play? Keep my hand in. It's been a while since I wrote that 3-act romantic comedy.

WIFE: Did you want cereal or toast? Quick!

MOH: Cereal, I think.

Her phone buzzes. She peeks at it, picks up the phone, reads and sighs deeply.

WIFE: Oh dear lord! Systems are down again! Bye, I have to get on a call.

MOH: Don't worry about me. I'll take care of my breakfast and coffee.

Wife sits down on a comfortable chair by the window, her laptop on her lap.

MOH makes coffee for her and sets the mug down next to her. He takes his own coffee mug down to his office and logs into his computer.

He starts typing "Bluetooth devices – They never sleep."

Something New

"You going out again, are you?"

Rob Fordham, his hand on the doorknob, paused, sighed and said, "I have to get the receiver back from the repair shop. I already told you that. It's ready for pick up."

"Oh, do you want me to come, then?"

Rob closed his eyes, careful not to turn around.

"If you can be ready in the next couple of minutes, sure, if you want to. It's not necessary. You won't come in to the store. It's cold out. If you're up to it, sure. I can't wait to too long, because they close at 6pm and it's already nearly five."

Susie Fordham was blonde, tall and unsure. She was in the stretch pants she usually wore around the house, with a fleece sweater.

"I should change, then. Right?" she said.

"If you want to. If you're not getting out of the car, there's no need to change, is there? Just throw on a jacket and let's go."

"You're right. I hate going into those electronics stores. They're boring."

"Ok, then why don't you stay home? I'll get this done and be back in an hour or so."

"But I want to come. Get some fresh air. I've been stuck in this house all day."

Rob suppressed a sigh.

"Susie, you're not going to get any fresh air. It's cold out, you'll sit in the car with the windows up and go there and come back. The only fresh air you'll get is from the walk door to the car, which is a distance of some twenty feet, coming and going."

"You're right. But then you'll go alone and come back alone. I thought you'd like some company."

"Yes. But, Susie, you're spending too much time trying to make up your mind. I don't have time and I can't make up your mind for you. You do this all the time. Are you coming or not?"

"I don't like the way you speak to me. Why are you always so angry, Rob?"

"OK – put on a jacket and let's go. Please? Now?"

Susie sat down on the couch.

"I don't want to", she said.

"Ok. I'll head out and get this done. See you in a bit."

Rob backed out of the driveway and roared down to the crossing. He waited for a break in traffic, cursing at the drivers who seemed to slow down and change lanes for the sole purpose of keeping him waiting there, expending his fuel.

He pulled into the parking lot in front of the store, almost knocking out the door of the car next to him, whose driver decided to step out at that precise moment.

He strode into the store, shaking his head, his teeth clenched. He dug into his pocket and flipped through the papers in his wallet. He found the receipt from the repair department and waited.

The elderly lady in front of him took her time to check that the repairs to her laptop had been done successfully. Satisfied, she packed it up carefully and stored it into the bag, making sure it was zipped correctly and completely. She reached into her large bag, extracted a large wallet holder and sorted through a large collection of cards, until she found the credit card she wanted to use.

Rob stared up at the ceiling as she dug into her bag again to find her reading glasses, carefully put them on and proceeded to enter her pin number. Finally, she took her receipt, collected all her belongings and turned around.

"I'm sorry for keeping you waiting", she said, turning slowly towards Rob.

"Oh no problem, take your time, please", said Rob, as he prepared to brush past her.

He handed the young man at the counter his receipt.

"I've got a receiver here for repair. I got a call it was done and ready for pickup."

"Yes, sir, let me check", said the service rep.

He typed away at the computer and said, "Yeah. I have it. Looks like the infrared sensor was replaced. Let me get it out of the back for you. I'll be right back."

He came back with a receiver and put it on the counter.

"There you are, sir. How would you like to pay?"

"Excuse me, is that receiver good?" said a voice behind him.

Rob flashed his credit card at the assistant and turned to see a lady looking at him expectantly.

"This one? Yes, a good brand, great sound, lots of inputs. Solid. Excuse me for a sec."

He turned to finish his payment.

"Yes. I accidentally bumped this against a corner of the table when I was moving, so killed a sensor. Otherwise, it's a very good buy."

"Oh ok. I'm in the market for something and it's so confusing in here."

"Can't go wrong with this brand! I can show you some options. But I just need to drop this off into the car first."

"Oh would you!? Please. Thank you. That would be wonderful."

Rob picked the receiver off the counter, and dropped into the boot of the car and found himself hurrying back into the store.

She was waiting for him, just inside the door, her tall figure topped by long blonde hair.

They spent the next forty five minutes, selecting, pickup and paying for a receiver.

"Oh, I can carry it", she cried.

"Oh, don't worry, I can handle it."

As he placed the box into her car, she said, "I don't know how to thank you. Can I buy you a drink?"

Rob hesitated a fraction.

"It's been a long day. Yes, I'd love to have a drink. Why not head over to Cooper's, it's conveniently placed just fifty metres away."

"I'm Sharon, by the way."

"Rob, is what my friends call me."

Once the drinks arrived, Rob raised his glass and said "Well, thanks. Here's to your new audio-visual experience!"

"Thanks so much. Now, I'll have to take it back and set it up somehow."

"It's quite easy! Colour match the cables and off you go."

"Oh, you don't understand. I have to hook this up to some old speakers. I don't know much about these things. See, my husband used to take care of all this. I never bothered to figure out how it was all done."

"Is your husband not there anymore? I'm sorry, it's not my intent to pry. It's ok if you don't want to share your life with a stranger you just met."

"Oh, it's ok. It's the same old story. We grew apart and we finally went our separate ways. All the paper work was done a while ago. The only thing he wanted was his receiver and his guitars. I got the house, the speakers and no A/V receiver."

Rob nodded.

"Sorry to hear that. Now you have a receiver, too."

"Yes, but nobody to set it all up."

"Would you want me to help? I can probably get away for a bit on Saturday morning..."

"Oh would you! No, I can't impose on you like that. You've already done so much."

"It was nothing much. So what time works for you? I can get there around eleven. Depending on the speakers and assuming there was already a receiver there, it shouldn't take too long."

Rob got home and dumped the receiver next to the TV. Susan watched him without saying a word.

The next morning, she was down early.

When Rob came down, dressed for work, she watched him pour out a coffee and said "I want a divorce."

Rob sipped his coffee, put some bread in the toaster, found a plate, buttered his toast and sat at the kitchen table.

"Did you hear me? I want a divorce."

"Yes. I'm very glad at your decisiveness. It's a change from the usual waffling. Sure. Get the papers ready. I'll sign them."

"Where were you so late, last night? The store closed at six and you didn't get here till after nine."

"Not that it matters, but I stopped for a drink. Will you have the papers ready this month?"

"I have to find a lawyer first. Should I ask Allie for hers? Or Linda. She said hers was really good."

"Ah, we're back. Well, can't help you there. I'm already a lawyer specializing in divorce cases, and I just retained myself. So, Susan, you'll have to ask Linda. Or Allie. Or, what's her name, Jen. Better find a good lawyer! Bye now, or I'll be late for work."

It was late summer the next year, when Rob and Susan signed the papers. Susan got the house. Rob took the sound system, his clothes and his collection of books and moved into an apartment a block away from the office,

That Christmas, Rob and Sharon went on a Mediterranean cruise. The cruise was eleven days long, covering Christmas and New Year. On New Year's Eve, just after midnight, Rob proposed and Sharon accepted.

"Oh isn't it beautiful? Fireworks at sea is such a great idea. You can really see the sparks and the lights here."

"Yes, no buildings to obstruct your view and no ambient light to dilute the spectacle."

"Oh Rob, this whole cruise, fireworks, everything was such good idea! I'm so glad to be here with you! This has been an absolutely great way to forget all the unpleasantness of the past two years. I love you so much!"

Rob held her close and kissed her.

"Thank you for being there. I'm so glad we met that day at the store. I hope I can live up to the promise of that time!"

New Year's Day was celebrated by a late brunch on board. There weren't too many early attendees. They were the older couples, who had retired to bed as soon as the fireworks had ended, or those who took an early rise as a requirement for a successful career.

Rob was up before Sharon. He brushed his teeth, and came back to bed so see Sharon awake and propped up against her pillow. He joined her.

"They have a brunch laid out it seems, according to his update they slipped under the door. You feel up to it?"

"I don't know. I'm so tired from last night, the trip, I can't believe we're engaged!"

"Well, congratulations, Sharon! You're a very lucky lady, indeed!"

"Hmmph! Smart aleck! Now, tell me, what do you want to do?"

"Me? I think, I'd like some coffee, some toast, some coffee, some home fries, some coffee, some bacon and then, maybe, a bit of coffee. Now what do you want to do?"

"I'm not sure. Coffee sounds good, but I was trying to cut back. Toast might work. Maybe some toast and a bit of coffee?"

"Well, let's go see what they have on the brunch menu!"

He flung himself out of bed.

Sharon carefully took out three blouses, two skirts and a pair of shorts.

"Now, what should I wear?"

"A t-shirt and those shorts."

"No, I think this pink top and that floral skirt."

"Yeah, that works, too."

"You're just saying that! Are you sure?"

"No, no! I like you in that skirt. I mean, I like you out of that skirt, too. Don't get me wrong!"

The wedding was a small affair. Neither of them wanted to make a big event out of their second marriages. They moved into Sharon's house. Rob kept the apartment, furnished and vacant.

Whenever, Sharon asked him about it, he replied, "Oh, I'm thinking about it. It comes in handy when I have to work late. My little law library is there, so it works like a great secondary office."

Plans for a honeymoon were marred by a sudden increase in Rob's caseload. Sharon, too, had a project that was in the final implementation stage.

Days went by swiftly and it wasn't until late spring that the idea of a vacation was brought up.

"Rob, don't you think we need some time off? I feel I could do with a holiday."

Rob, busy reading his notes, said, "Uh huh. Organize something, for mid June, I should be done with this by then."

"Should we go to the beach? I'd like that."

"Sure. Beach is fine. Whatever you like."

"Uh, but we went on the cruise. The beach would be more of the same. How about something new?"

Rob looked up and carefully put away the file.

"When you say 'something new', maybe pick the mountains, then. We haven't done mountains."

Sharon stuck her lower lip out.

"Hmm, but mountains are so tiring! And then we'll likely have to get boots and carry that extra weight."

"Good point. Beach, then."

"Oh, I don't know. Should I check with Alanna? She does a lot of vacations now that she's single, and has all that money Steve left her."

"Yeah. Ask her. Maybe, ask Marianne."

"Should I? I mean, she has so much to say. Maybe, I will. Or, Judy! Yes, Judy. Now why didn't I think of her?"

"I suggest ask all of them. Then decide."

"But what if they all give conflicting ideas? How does one decide?"

Rob picked up his file.

"You'll figure something out. Just make sure that it's something new. And pray, the something new isn't the something old."

"What do you mean?"

"I don't know. Can I finish this, please? I need to get the notes out tomorrow morning."

"I'd like something new, actually! What a great idea, Rob!"

Rob grunted.

The silence lasted for five minutes.

Sharon put away her phone and said, "Judy says the beach is a great idea. But I'm not sure I want to go to the beach. I want something new, something different."

"So do I, Sharon, so do I. But what's new and what's different? You figure it out. I'm off to bed."

The next morning, Sharon had the laptop out and was browsing through vacation options.

"It says here, Italy is a great place. But we were in the Mediterranean last time. How about Portugal?"

"Works for me! Never been there, so yeah. Book it."

"Or, we could go to the Grand Canyon."

"Haven't been there, either, so sure!"

"I'm not sure it appeals to me, actually. Too rustic and in the middle of nowhere."

"Los Angeles? If you want people around you, or Vegas? Not a big fan of Vegas, but if you want, we can go there."

"I'm really having a hard time making up my mind about where I want to go."

"Talk to your friends. Alanna, Judy or Marianne. Maybe they have some ideas for something new."

"I don't know that something new is always better."

Rob, his hand on the door, said "I'm going for a run. You work it out. I'm good with whatever takes your fancy. See you in a bit."

"On second thought, something new would be nice. Let me talk to the girls and see what ideas they have."

Rob shut the door behind him, put his headphones on and took off down the street.

Fish for Breakfast

The afternoon sun disappeared as if it had been switched off. A sharp wind came whipping in from the southwest. Grey clouds scudded across the city hanging lower and lower. The first few spattering raindrops grew into a sharp and heavy shower. The storm swept through the city in a vicious display of power and fury. Weak branches split and fell, bushes bent over under the strength of the rain and wind, flowers lost the petals.

Aindrila turned from the last window and sighed. She had mixed feelings about these *kalbaishakis,* these sudden late spring storms, which appeared over the crowded city of Calcutta with barely a warning and left as suddenly as it had come.

She loved the rain, the cooler temperatures, and the smell of the electricity in the atmosphere. If only one didn't have to rush around shutting windows, taking in the drying laundry and the general air of battening down, she could enjoy the storm.

This Thursday, the storm outside was a distraction from the storm inside.

Ever since she had picked up the piece of paper from just inside the bathroom, Aindrila had been seething.

How dare he! She hadn't answered Neil's usual 11am call to check on her as he usually did. Her mind was in a whirl. She sat down and read the words again.

AJESH SHARMA

Fish! I hate fish. I hate fish for breakfast. Who has fish for breakfast? It's all very well for those Brits to sing "Could we have kippers for breakfast, mummy dear, mummy dear". Porridge made from scratch was the only thing one really needed. What was wrong with simple parathas, maybe toast, even whole-wheat toast, or rye or sourdough to change it up?

"Just wait till he gets home! He's going to get dry toast, with no butter or jam for dinner!" Aindrila spoke out through clenched teeth.

As the storm blew itself out, Aindrila locked up the house and sallied forth to the local market. She carefully counted out the money, after intense haggling and brought her catch home.

She spent the afternoon in the kitchen, occasionally looking up the iPad propped on the counter.

Neil arrived a little later than normal, 7 PM instead of the 6:30 PM he usually managed.

"Traffic was a nightmare. Trees have fallen and the signals are out across Alipore Road and Judges Court Road crossing. That was a bad storm."

Aindrila took the umbrella from him and took it out to the verandah.

"You know, umbrellas are the most useless invention ever", said Neil, taking off his shoes and socks.

"What do you mean?" said Aindrila.

"If there's a hint of breeze, the rain blows under it. Any gust will flip it inside out. Your pants are wet, anyway. And worst of all, once it is wet, there's no way to take care of it without getting wet anyway."

"On top of which, you lose about four a year", said Aindrila.

"Well, you keep buying and insisting I carry them! Why don't you learn? Anyway, what's for dinner?"

"I have a special surprise for you."

"Oh! What?"

"Go and get out of those wet things, first. Do you want some tea or go straight to dinner?"

"Well, if it's a surprise for me, I'd rather just get to dinner. It's late anyway", Neil's voice was muffled by the towel he was using to wipe his head.

He walked in, dressed in his pyjamas and a t-shirt that said "Gone Fishing!" across the front.

He peeked into the kitchen and saw Aindrila busy readying dinner. He found the TV remote and switched it on. He stood there watching a report on the days rains. Some of the poorer parts of town which had poor drainage were flooded. Shots of people standing or walking through ankle deep water flitted by.

"Turn it off and let's have dinner", said Aindrila carrying a casserole to the table, "Get the big pan in from the kitchen for me, please."

"Yes, ma'am", he said.

"Smells good! Let's see what we got here."

He sat down and took the cover off the pan.

"Oooh, is that the surprise? Looks like potato curry!"

"I made some *pakoras* with the last of the chickpea flour. We have to get some more when we go this weekend."

"What kind? Potato, onions and eggplant, too! Oh, and *luchis*? Oh yeah! This is a surprise. You must love me very much. What have I done right to deserve this?"

"Oh, you know. I thought it would be nice."

"Well, I'm not complaining. Thanks for this! Now shut up and let me eat!"

After dinner, they watched Aindrila's favorite show, a documentary where men and women went to impossible lengths to carefully dig out bones of prehistoric animals from hard to reach lands. Neil checked the sports news and the usual fare of politicians throwing mud at each other.

The next morning, Neil's breakfast was an English muffin, toasted with peanut butter and jam. A bowl of cereal lay ready. He ate in silence, checking his watch as he ate. Then he was into his shoes and out of the door.

Aindrila had just finished clearing up when the front doorbell rang. She peeked through the eyehole and opened the door.

"Hi, Ratna! Come on in! I was just putting the breakfast away."

"I was wondering if you wanted to go shopping. I need to go and get some stuff and I know we'd talked about going."

"Yes, give me a couple of minutes for a quick shower and we can go. Maybe we can grab some lunch too?"

She hurried off to take a shower. Ratna wandered around the living room, peering at the photograph of Neil and Aindrila at their wedding. Neil looked lost and Aindrila seemed shyly happy. Her eye fell upon the piece of paper next to the photo.

She read the scrawling and very untidy handwriting. Her eyes widened, she shrugged and placed the paper back.

"Is it going to rain? Should I carry an umbrella?" asked Aindrila.

"I'm not carrying one. I'm just going to lose it anyway. I don't think those things are useful at all."

"That's what Neil says, too. I make sure he carries one, though."

"Hmm, so, you either love him a lot or you really hate him. Which is it?" asked Ratna?

"Don't be silly! Let's go."

They took the elevator down and walked along to the crossing. Ratna hailed a cab in that imperious way she had and soon they were threading their way down to the centre of town.

"Here let me pay", said Aindrila.

Ratna brushed her off and the two got out and walked into the mall. They spent their time strolling around the multiple floors. They tried on clothes and missed not a single shoe shop.

Tired and laden with bags, they stood in the middle of the food court, scanning the choices available. Aindrila opted for a Chinese combo and Ratna bought a sandwich with a bag of chips. They found a table and sat down, making sure their bags were tucked away under table.

"Chowmein looks good. Maybe, I should have got some too", said Ratna.

"Here have some of mine. Go ahead."

"Nope. You're a very good natured and kind person, you know. I can't take advantage of you."

"No, no!"

"Yes, yes. You do let people take advantage of you. That husband of yours, who you love so much, he treats you like a doormat. You're always there. He just takes you for granted."

"Oh no. He's very kind. He works quite hard. I'm not working right now, so what's the harm in supporting him?"

"Are you going to work any time?"

"Yes, I'm just waiting to finish this online certification course. Then I will start applying. Hopefully, it won't take too long."

"But you do all the cooking. Does he help at all?"

"I don't really want him messing around in the kitchen. He'll just make a mess."

"Well, I hope you're a good cook."

"He has little choice!"

"I saw that note. Is that him complaining about fish?" asked Ratna.

"Oh, you saw that! Yeah! Apparently, he felt strongly enough to write it down. I don't think he expected me to see it, though. He's not the type."

"Oh, I don't know, Andy, maybe he is passive aggressive and you're just not willing to acknowledge that."

"Well, I do think that fish is a bit of a jump for many people."

"Why do you say that?"

"Fish isn't the easiest thing in the world. Look, first catching the fish. Time consuming, no guarantee of the catch, it's quality or quantity."

"Ok, I agree! Fishing is hard and takes a lot of time. And, as you said, there are no guarantees. So what?"

"Well, buying fish is an art form in itself, right? You have to be there at the right time, identify freshness. And, then comes the hardest part – the valuation, the bargaining and the final price."

Ratna broke in with, "It's still pretty passive aggressive to write it down."

"I disagree. It's actually very nice of him. He didn't complain, whine or make a big song or dance over it. He let off a little private steam, so what?"

"You're just madly in love with him, aren't you?"

"I don't know about love. You know, now that I quit my job to sit at home and write, he's ok with it. And I do appreciate that.

Besides, fish is such an interesting thing to write about! I think I will write an article about it."

"What do you mean, it's interesting? Fish is just fish!"

"I'm not so sure. You know, that's one thing, I noticed at work. The conversation around the price of fish is always a great start to any conversation, and then you can go on to the quality, politics, policy and there is a collective shaking of heads, and a general air of being in the same club somehow, and a camaraderie develops so fast that way."

"What rubbish! Are you saying that you talked about fish at work?"

"I was a Business Analyst!"

"What does that have to do with it?"

"Ok, my job was to meet with loads of people and understand what they wanted. Then write it down in a way that everyone could understand it. See, that's where my writing skills came in. Having a degree in English helped me write it down correctly in good English. Good English got me into a trouble a lot. So I quit."

"So you got into trouble for talking about fish? You're crazy!"

"Ah see, it's a complicated thing."

"Ok, so uncomplicate it for me!"

"There's no such word! Uncomplicate. Make it simpler, is what you should be using. That's another rant altogether! How much time do you have?"

"Ooh, I have all day to listen to this! Go ahead, this should be good!"

Aindrila took a sip of her large helping of Diet Coke.

"Consultants were the bane of my existence. They worked with executives, and what they actually did was put down what the executive wanted in a manner that appealed to the executive's vanity."

Ratna cocked her head.

"How did they do this? Well, to understand this you have to understand where executives seemingly got their ideas."

"And where would that be?"

"Golf courses, seminars that only executives attended, usually in Las Vegas, or some other hotspot. Why did only executives attend these dos? Well, budget constraints, mostly. So the poor little grains of left over rice, like me, were cut off from all training courses and other opportunities that may have contributed to our skills and learning."

"Can I say that you sound extraordinarily bitter?"

"Realist, me. Not bitter, just jaded and cynical."

"Ok! Go on!"

"So! Some executive would have been off playing golf with someone who triggered some need that didn't exist, which nobody, not even the executive could truly express. But, hey, some guy who seemed to know about it had appealed to the executive's vanity, as I said, or opened up an opportunity."

Aindrila made the quotation mark with her fingers as she said the word 'opportunity'.

"The executive would then come back to the office and set off his team of followers, sycophants and diligent workers to produce the sales materials that would satisfy the executive enough to take to his superiors for the money and approvals needed."

"I'm finding this utterly fascinating!"

"So then this money and approval usually meant the hiring of consultants, because they didn't trust their own staff to have brains. Which is odd, because they hired these people, apparently, for their brains. Anyway, the consultant hordes come in. The executive would brief them on his idea. Then the consultants would work on producing a presentation full of dials, charts, showing market research, and using words they dreamed up in their energy drink driven all night binges. Words like 'uncomplicate' instead of 'simplify' and the one I used to hate the most, 'degrow' for 'reduce'.

"What? Degrow?"

"I kid you not!"

Ratna smacked her forehead.

"I, also, have a degree in English. Though, you have the knack for storytelling, which I don't. I get your grief!"

"Thanks. But back to fish! So, then the project is approved, after the consultants have spent a million dollars and produced thirty two editions of ye famouse presentation. Finally, it would come to someone like me to talk to the poor dears who were going to have to figure out what was required, how it would work and how to develop it. And, thus, we come to fish. Fish is a great analogy for the whole business analysis thing. Just like a fisherman sits patiently for countless hours at the river, or sea, to catch something worthwhile, a business analyst sits patiently in countless meetings to catch something that looks like a problem someone wants to solve or a need they want to fulfill. Or at worst, figure out how to actually address whatever pea brained idea that was sponsored by the powers that be. The fisherman uses bait, food, worms, so that the fish come nibble at it to satisfy their curiosity. The good Business Analyst learns to talk about fish, to put them at their ease, draw them out, slowly and surely, into explaining what the hell it is they thought they wanted. Usually, it would turn out that what they wanted would not solve the problem anyway, because the problem itself had never been defined in clear terms."

"You are really something! How do you even think of such things!"

"I was bored out my mind, Ratna! You lucky thing never had to face the sheer futility of business needs and problems. It all came down to one thing, in the end."

"And that was?"

"Futility. They'd go through endless repeats of the same cycle of failures. Deem successful all those that were sponsored by the ones they loved and brush all those that they didn't like under the carpet or out of the door."

"Yes. That I understand. Those you love can do no wrong and those you can't stand can do no right. That's a fundamental law of life. But, hang on, what about the other folks there in the team. You have project managers, and the people who actually build stuff, test it and package it. What do they do?"

"Project managers have been reduced to paper pushers. Almost clipboard checklist specialists. They've been told not to think for themselves but simply harangue people with lists of things that someone up top said, six months ago, should be done, never mind that those things don't make any sense now that everyone else knows or should know better."

"Yes. Life does keep changing and we can't always go by what we thought it should be months ago. That's common sense."

"Ah, common sense! Well, there isn't any being applied. It is in very short supply. Someone somewhere figured out that this was the wrong thing to do, so there are people who sell a new way of looking at things. Short attention periods. They call them sprints, they changed the names of project managers to scrum masters and everyone suddenly became agile. The truth is, nothing's changed.

The same lack of common sense prevails, changes are frowned upon and flexibility is abhorred. Or so it seemed to me."

"But if they recognize that it's not working, shouldn't someone..."

"Well, in my opinion, the people up there got to where they are under the older system. What incentive will they have to adopt a new method, one they don't understand, when they became successful by fully exploiting the old one?"

"Yes. I get that. Nobody likes change."

"It's not change itself. They're worried that some upstart will take over. They worry about losing relevancy after they've spent twenty years becoming familiar with the old methods. Think about it. You're middle aged, doing what was set up, diligently, like clockwork, on cruise control, driving along a road you've driven on to the point where you don't need to think and suddenly the car you're in has changed, all the controls are different, the roads are twisty and unknown and you have to navigate through this, all the while people going tsk tsk and exhorting you to learn this wonderful new way. It's not wonderful to you! You could schedule your time, go home at the same time, you were the expert. Now suddenly, some young twenty something comes along, treats you like some ancient dinosaur who is beyond repair and should have been removed from the scene. Indeed, that young person is already probably working on a plan to remove you. How would you feel?"

"Wow! Good then that I'm an idle housewife, from a well-to-do family, married into a family with wealth, so never had to work and experience such things."

"I'm not complaining. It gave me a wealth of stuff to put in my articles and hopefully a novel. So all is not yet lost!"

As they put away up their now empty containers and headed back home, Aindrila was silent, letting Ratna chatter away about all sorts of things. She nodded and said "ah, right" at select intervals, but otherwise took no part in the conversation.

As she sat down with her afternoon cup of tea, she replayed Ratna's comment in her head.

She hadn't exactly come from a poor family. She'd been to the same school as Ratna, had the same opportunities to learn. Why, then, did she decided to work? Especially, as it became clear now, that Neil's work was more than sufficient to keep them financially secure with plenty of opportunity to save for retirement.

There were no children to look after, unlike Ratna, who had two. So that didn't add anything to the expense column.

Yet, Aindrila was bothered by what Ratna had said. Why did she need to work? What was work? Other than giving you money to survive. All it seemed to do was increase your propensity to consume which allowed corporates to create more, to give you more work, so you could never escape that circle of life.

It was slavery, pure and simple. They conned you into the rate race at work, so you'd forget to dream, and start believing that moving up the ladder was what you really, really wanted, when in actual fact what you wanted to do was create. Maybe write a novel, travel, see the world, observe, and enjoy the differences in foods, architectures, ambience and languages. There was so much to do and most people seemed to trap themselves into the mindless and endless chase for other people's dreams.

Aindrila was convinced.

She sat down at the desk, fired up her laptop and started to write the book she now knew she was supposed to write.

A Spectacular Wedding

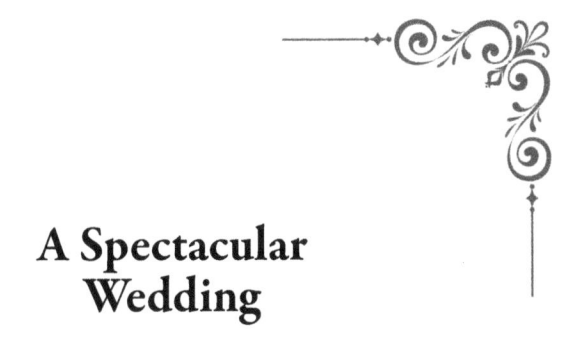

It had to be in June and it had to be spectacular.

Brittany made that abundantly clear at the first meeting with Stephanie. It had to be outdoors, so the weather had to be good, July and August were too hot and September was unpredictable. June was the perfect time. Brittany wanted it to be special, spectacular and something that would leave a lasting impression on those attending.

Stephanie said, "Now, this is our first meeting. It's more about introductions and setting expectations. Just so we know where we are and where we want to be. As we go through, we'll take a look at settings, people, food, drinks, and the music choices. We'll also take a look at seating arrangements, decorations and a host of other things."

"I'm expecting you to take charge of all of it. But, I want to you to know that I have some very interesting ideas and I'd like you to take those on and do what you have to do to make them happen."

"Well, Brittany, may I suggest that we put some stuff down on paper. I'll put together a template for you. I would certainly love to hear your ideas. It is your wedding, after all, so you need to be comfortable with everything. I want to make sure that your ideas are incorporate as best we can. Over the next few weeks and months, we will create a plan, ensure we're tracking to it and we can modify if we need to. You should share these with Ben, as well, make sure he's comfortable, as well."

"I don't want my plans to change! I know what I want, and your job is to make sure I get it! Ben doesn't want to interfere, he said."

Stephanie had heard this before, so was unfazed by it. She smoothly transitioned into the planning exercise.

Over the weeks, it became clear that Ben was just her fiancé, and thus had very little say in the matter. Besides, he was lucky to have managed to get Brittany to say yes to his awkward proposal.

"Cute. He was so cute! He cleared his throat, went down on one knee in the middle of the ball game. Everyone turned to see! It was on the big screens all through! I had to say yes! I mean, he is so....cute!"

Stephanie had no comment. She hadn't met Ben yet and she was experienced enough to know that every bride to be was convinced her fiancé was cute, or handsome, or sweet.

Slowly but surely, she led Brittany through the process of organizing the wedding of her dreams.

"I want it to be unforgettable! And spectacular." was her refrain.

Stephanie made notes of Brittany's ideas. It became apparent, as Stephanie knew it would, that Brittany's ideas were silly, pretentious or downright selfserving. She had given no thought about the guests, and how they would be treated.

It was normal, everyday stuff for Stephanie.

She suggested ideas, carefully and expertly steered Brittany off the untenable notions of a "grand wedding."

It helped that Brittany's dad was there to write checks, because there were a lot of them. Luckily, he could afford them. He was in equal parts gruff and dismissive of Stephanie, who didn't really care. She took the checks, deposited them, paid decorators, caterers, bar tenders, videographers, photographers, drivers and other staff.

She still had not been introduced to the elusive fiancée, Ben. He was either busy or not considered important enough to attend the planning sessions.

Alone at home, she thought about her own elusive Ben. He was Ben Hutton, too, just like Brittany's Ben.

Ben, who had disappeared shortly after their trip to Antigua, where on the beach, he had proposed to Stephanie. Two days after their return, he had gone on a business trip to South Africa. She had kissed him at the gate and waved goodbye as he hurried off, his laptop bag across his shoulder down to the plane.

That was the last time she had seen him or heard from him. A few days of silence and she wondered where he was. It was then that she realized that he had never spoken about his work, his friends, his family. They had spent all their time at restaurants and pubs, or at her apartment. All she had was a selfie taken shortly after the engagement. Other than that, she knew nothing about Ben, if that was his name.

No, his name was Ben. She'd seen the credit card. Benjamin Hutton. She had looked for that name online. Plenty of B Huttons showed up, but none of them looked or read like they were Ben.

That was two years ago. Stephanie busied herself with building her wedding planning business. She dated nobody and met with barely anyone. Nobody knew about her two weeks fling with Ben, their holiday and the engagement.

Brittany called the next morning.

"Hi Stephanie! I need to see you. Can you come over? Eleven?"

Stephanie made sure her laptop had all the updated files, before she left the apartment. When Brittany called to meet her, it was usually a change of mind or heart, or another "lovely" idea. It usually meant going over the existing approved plans, so she could convey what that meant in terms of cost and time.

She waited in the living room they normally used at Brittany's house, with her laptop open, a notebook and pen beside it. She scanned the plans, the website that was now up and running.

Brittany walked in, and said, "Hi Stephanie! I want you to meet Ben!"

Stephanie looked up and was half out of her seat when she stopped, froze and sat down again.

Britanny said, "Ben, this is Stephanie. She's helping us put the wedding together. You know that website and sample cards and photos I showed you? She's the one."

Stephanie collected her thoughts, put a smile on her face, and her hand out to Ben.

"Hi. Good to meet you, finally!"

Ben was tall, as tall as she remembered. His hair grew in an unruly manner across a scalp that seemed to have a bald patch on one side. It was difficult to see under the hair, but Stephanie was sure there was a clean patch under it.

He stuck his hand out, and said "Nice to meet you! Britt's been showing me the stuff you've been working on. I'm very impressed."

"Thank you! I hope to see you guys have a wonderful wedding day. And all the best wishes for your life ahead."

Ben had his head cocked to one side. He was on the verge of sticking his finger out in a gesture of confused recognition. He was about to say something when Brittany took over and started talking about the types of flowers and would the colours match the dresses of the bridesmaids.

Throughout the discussion, Ben didn't lose that bemused look on his face.

As Stephanie finally shut down the laptop, she said, "Well, looks like that's it for now. I'll make the updates and send you the final numbers. Just mail the check."

She stood up and shook hands.

Ben said, "I'll show you out."

Brittany said goodbye and went off inside. Ben held the door open for Stephanie and the walked down the steps to her car.

She opened the trunk, put her bag away and turned to see her standing watching her.

"You must excuse me. But I have to know. I am sure I have seen you somewhere before."

"I don't think so. Different circles and I don't go out much."

She shrugged.

"Where was your last holiday?" he asked.

Stephanie drew herself up and said clearly, "Antigua. Was there for a quick three day getaway."

"Antigua? Where's that? Oh no, wait, the Caribbean. Don't think I've been there, but I don't have all my memory back, yet."

"Well, it's not important. So I'll see you around, I guess. It would be nice for you to take a more involved role in the whole wedding planning. Sometimes, Brittany could use some help."

"Ah yes. Pardon me, but I have, as I alluded to there, some difficulty in focusing sometimes. That's why she doesn't want to bother me. But I try! I'll try harder! Thank you for all you're doing."

Stephanie drove off in a mass of confused emotions.

It was Ben. She was sure now. But she didn't remember the bald patch, or the unruly hair. His hands, too, seemed to have a different feel to it. They felt harder and at the same time, there was a quiet tremor.

It was Saturday morning when the phone rang. It was an unknown caller. Stephanie didn't answer it, but sat with her legs up on the couch, watching the morning news, sipping coffee.

The phone rang twice more and then a text message showed up.

Hi Stephanie. This is Ben. Got your number from Brittany. I'd like to talk to you. When you get a chance please call this number.

Stephanie finished her coffee. Sat down with her laptop and updated her own business website, adding testimonials and editing pages. Two hours later, she changed into her running gear and went for a run.

There were no more texts or calls from Ben. She showered, made some chicken curry and had it with sourdough bread.

Late afternoon, she texted Ben.

Oh, hi, Ben. Sorry couldn't answer earlier. Running errands and things got busy. You can call me now or tomorrow morning, perhaps?

She saw the message was delivered and read. The phone rang.

"Stephanie. Ben here. Thanks for returning my message. Can we meet and talk? Please, I need to clear up a few things."

"Hi Ben, sure. When do you want to meet? Monday?"

"Can we do tomorrow morning? Is there a coffee shop where we can sit, have a coffee and breakfast?"

"Uh, Hmm. Let me see. There's a coffee shop down by Queen St and Thomas. It's quiet, they have some seating and they do bagels and croissants."

"Would nine be too early? Or late?"

"Nine's fine. It's called the Lisboa Bakery. I'll bring the laptop so we can go over the plans."

"Thank you. See you tomorrow then."

Stephanie chewed two of her special gummy bears and went to sleep early.

When she awoke, it was just past seven. She had a cup of coffee to shake off the last effects of the gummy bears and at eight thirty, she left her apartment.

As she walked, her mind went back to the four weeks, those four weeks when Ben had been in her life. It seemed, now, as if she had dreamed it. It couldn't possibly been real. It was the rooftop party, after Ashleigh's wedding. Ashleigh, warm as a teddy bear, had insisted that she come.

"I mean, come on! Look at how the wedding went! It was like a dream and you made it possible! You have to come."

So she had. She'd been leaning against the wall, away from the lights and the dancing, sipping her glass of wine, when she became aware that someone had take up a position next to her.

"Hi."

Those were his first words.

"Hi", is what she said.

"Not enjoying the party, eh?"

"Um, the important thing is Ashleigh and Evan are. Look at them!"

"Yeah. They are, aren't they?"

"Uh huh."

"You're one of Ashleigh's friends?"

"Not really. I don't really know anyone here."

"Oh, like me! What's your excuse for being here? Mine is quite simple. I'm the plus 1 for one of Ashleigh's friends."

"Mine is even simpler. I'm the wedding planner. So for me, it's purely a business interest."

"Ah, so we're both strangers here! Well, let me tell you that my name is Ben. I don't live here, too cold for me. No, I currently live on the west coast, where we get rained on all the time. I guess that's the price we pay."

"Oh, I moved here a few years ago. I was studying to be a pharmacist. I'm from out east."

"A bit a change from pharmacy to wedding plans? How did that happen?"

"I drifted into it. One day I was graduating from college and the next thing I knew I was a wedding planner!"

"Funny how things happen, isn't it. There you were..... let me guess, Linda or Lorraine?"

"Oh sorry. Stephanie."

"Ah, now we're not strangers any more! I'm Ben. You are Stephanie."

"Nice to meet you, Ben."

The conversation moved smoothly, with an easy familiarity. The next day he made breakfast for her, using her kitchen with ease, as he assembled coffee, eggs and bacon.

Ben, it turned out, had arrived in the city from Cape Town. He had been in Vancouver for three months, working on a project. The only person he knew was a friend his cousin knew. The friend worked with Ashleigh, had recently broken up and needed a plus one for Ashleigh's wedding.

Stephanie's steps were measured as she walked towards the Lisboa Bakery. She didn't want to appear to be anxious or hurried. As she turned the final corner, she saw him standing at the door, peering in.

She slowed down and said "Hi".

He turned to her.

"Oh, hi! I was wondering whether I should go in and wait or wait outside."

"Let's go in and find a table."

Once inside he carefully inspected the croissants and banana bread options, selected one of each. She opted for a coffee, black with no sugar. He got himself a cappuccino.

He took a tentative sip of his cappuccino.

"Thank you for meeting me. I really wanted to talk with you. Friday was a bit of a shock for me, seeing you. Again."

"Again? Have we met before?"

"My memory isn't what it used to be. Apparently, the knock on my head and my time with doctors tells me it isn't what it used to be. It's getting better and every once in a while something happens and another chunk of some forgotten memory comes rushing back."

"Head? You had a head injury?"

"Listen. Let me talk for a bit and some of the hazier bits will become clearer. This coffee is helping I think."

"Have the croissant and take it slowly", she said.

He took a bit and chewed it, his eyes not leaving hers.

"Talk to me", he said, "Tell me who you are. Tell me about yourself. Tell about Antigua. You said it was the last holiday you were on."

She took a deep breath.

"Not a whole lot to tell, actually. I live alone. I have a small apartment a few blocks away. I'm a wedding planner. The bit about Antigua being the last holiday isn't true, I suppose. It was nearly two years ago. I don't know why I said Antigua. I've taken short holidays, long weekends, just lazing through small towns by myself. Never more than a few days. Sometimes, I've had weddings out of town, so I've added days by myself."

"Antigua. They have beaches there. Lots of them. A hotel with private suites on the beach. Light grey walls, colorful paintings and bedcovers."

She didn't say anything.

"Does that mean something to you? There's got to be a reason why you said that. And it has triggered something. That description, why is that image in my head."

"Have some more croissant. Or that banana bread. It seems to help."

He chomped away and started talking with his mouth full of a mix of croissant and banana bread.

"You know, the doctors said, my memory would come back slowly. I was in Cape Town, luckily, so my parents were there to look after me."

"Tell me about the accident."

"Well, I came back to Cape Town and the taxi I was in skidded off the road and hit a tree and turned over. The taxi driver was killed. I must have bumped my head hard against something. I was in a coma for four days. When I came out of it, I had no idea who I was, where I was and why I was where I was. They refused to let me out of the hospital for another two weeks. I had to learn how to walk, talk, even and do simple things like feed myself. The motor skills actually didn't take long to come back. I sound perfectly normal now. Except, I don't recall many things from the past. There are some flashes and then periods of emptiness. It's a little frustrating, because people think I'm rude. But the truth is, I can't recall who they are, why they're talking to me and how they seem to know things I cannot remember."

Stephanie drained her coffee.

"Stephanie. Your name. Somewhere in my head, that is supposed to mean something."

"Antigua", she said.

"Antigua. That's what triggered this flash. The beach, the hotel. There's a girl. Tall brunette, round metal frame sunglasses."

Stephanie pulled a pair of sunglasses out of her bag and put them on.

"Like these?"

He dropped the slice of banana bread and fell back.

"Oh my god! Stephanie!! It was you!"

"It was me? Are you sure? Where did you see me last?"

Ben put his hands in head, elbows on the table. A low moan escaped him.

"What did I do? Antigua! My god, Stephanie. You were the girl in Antigua with me. I have been there. I was with you. Something happened there..."

"Something did. You are right. You and I spent a few days there."

"And? What did I do?"

"You sure you want to know?"

"Please, Stephanie, help me. Tell me what happened."

So she did. She told him about meeting at Ashleigh's party, spending the night together, the next few days together, the whirlwind trip to Antigua, laughing, holding hands and running through the waves on the sandy beach.

"The last day we were there, you proposed. And you didn't even have a ring. We cut up a napkin and made do! Do you remember?"

"Oh my god! Stephanie! What have I done! Oh no! Poor Stephanie! You must have cursed me for just disappearing like that!"

"Well, I did think I had judged you wrong, or I had made an error of judgement. I was so enjoying myself that I never stopped to ask who you were, what you did, where you lived. So when you disappeared I had nowhere to ask questions. I didn't even know who your cousin was."

"Is there a park or a place where we can talk without people staring at us?"

"My apartment."

They sat there talking, remembering, and crying over a past that had passed by them.

When his phone rang, he wiped the tears from his eyes and said, "Hi, Britt. Sorry I forgot, can you make your way there? And I'll meet you there. I won't have time to pick you up now. Sorry!"

He shut down the phone and said, "Stephanie, my dear Stephanie. I have to go. For now. But I know who you are. I know where you live. I won't forget you Stephanie, that's a promise. I have to talk to Brittany and I'll call you right after."

She watched him go out of the door, stop and turn at the top of the stairs. She waited for him to leave, then shut the door, threw herself on the bed and lay there, alternating between sobs and sniffs.

Stephanie spent the rest of the Sunday, sitting up in bed with the laptop, alternating between watching videos of monasteries in Spain, Portugal and remote parts of Europe and crying.

There was no news from Ben. The phone lay next to her, as dumb as a paperweight, but without its efficiency.

A fitful night's sleep was cut short by the phone waking up in a display of frantic anxiety.

It was Brittany.

"Hi Stephanie, I need to meet today. Something has happened and we need to figure out what it means for us."

"Uh, Brittany, does this have to do with the wedding uh plans?"

"Just come over, I'll explain. Ben is being very difficult and I need to talk to you."

Stephanie had barely pushed the doorbell when it was jerked open and Brittany, dressed in torn jeans, a t-shirt that said "Back to a troubled future", and flip-flops. The vision of the normally immaculately dressed Brittany clad thus, made Stephanie blink as she hesitantly walked into the room.

And there he was. Ben stuck his hand out to Stephanie. She shook it very briefly and turned to Brittany.

"Brittany, I don't know what's happened, but can I explain?"

"There's nothing for you to explain! It's this guy. He's having cold feet and wants to cancel the wedding!"

"What?"

"Look, Britt, I didn't mean...."

Ben got no further before Brittany cut him off.

"No, you look, Ben. This wedding is going to happen. I've spent weeks here with Stephanie. She's done a great job. I'm not going to let you back away from it. Especially with some stupid reason."

Stephanie said, "Can we all sit down, please. I need to, at least. I'm trying to understand what's happened so I can figure out what I need to do."

"It's very simple. Ben here wants to cancel the wedding because he wants to go home, apparently for some business reason. He can't explain why it can't be held up until after the wedding. The wedding is ten days away. Why can't this wait?"

Ben said, "Britt, I told you. I need to get this thing done, otherwise there are going to be difficulties."

"Penalties? It's going to cost you? How much, Ben? How much? You have any idea how much I'm spending on this wedding? How much has already been spent?"

"I understand, Britt. I'll pay for it all. But I have to go away."

"Have you lost your mind? There's no way in hell I'm going to let you get away with this. This wedding will happen, like it or not. It's going to be big, spectacular and something people will remember. You can go away after it's done."

"Go away? If this goes through, and I go away, I may never come back, you understand? I don't like the way you're talking or thinking right now. It seems the show is more important than us. How will our relationship work if we're going to start like this?"

"Don't know. Don't care. It's happening and I want to remember it always and I want my friends to remember it always as well. After that, I don't even care what you do. I'm going to have my day."

Ben threw his hands up in a display of exasperated despair.

Stephanie said, "Wait, let me understand. You're saying Ben wants to call it off because he has to go away on a business trip? Is that the reason?"

Ben said, "It's very important. I can't be at this wedding."

As Brittany and Ben both started talking at the same time in raised voices, Stephanie got up and walked to the door.

"Brittany", she said, "I have to go and figure things out. I'm sure you have to as well. Maybe, if we can all take a step back and think things through. Also, I'm wondering if I should speak with Ben alone. Maybe, sort through things from his perspective and then we can regroup, so to speak."

"There's no need. This wedding is taking place ten days from now. The end."

"Ok, Brittany, I understand your perspective on this", said Stephanie, "I'm going to take Ben away and understand what he's trying to do. Then, maybe, I can get us all back together figure how we move forward. Ben, come with me. Brittany, you stay on here. I'm taking him away from the house."

Ben followed Stephanie out of the house.

"We'll take my car, Ben. I don't trust you to drive."

"No, I don't want to leave my car here. Why don't we both drive ourselves out to wherever you have in mind?"

They drove back to Stephanie's apartment.

"Coffee. I could do with some", she said, throwing her keys on the little tray next to the door.

"You, I could do with some of you, or all of you", he said, enfolding her in his arms.

She put her arms around his neck, and they stood there, their lips locked. Then she pulled away.

"Ben, we have to figure out what to do! We can't waste time."

Ben's phone pinged.

"It's her. Long text, let me see what she has to say."

He leaned with his butt against the table and read the whole thing, scrolling up and down to make sure he collected all that Brittany had to say.

"Ok. Here's the deal. She wants the wedding. Or she'll sue for breach of promise. Which she's likely to win."

"So we're done then."

"She also says, she wants the wedding day to be perfect, spectacular and something everyone will remember. She's not giving up on that. After the wedding, she expects a honeymoon as planned, but that's optional."

"Oh, I forgot about that part. Ben, just when I found you, I have to lose you again! This is the saddest part of my sad life so far."

Ben cocked his head to one side and looked at her. She had her head in her hands, slumped on the little couch. She looked up, her eyes glistening, her head shaking.

"There's always a way, Stephanie. We have to think. She wants a wedding. A big spectacular one that everyone will remember. The rest is optional. She wants that day. Let's give her that. Let's make it spectacular! Something she will remember and all her friends will remember for the rest of their lives! Come on! Think!"

They sat through pizza, a six-pack of beer for him and bottle of merlot for her. Finally, they threw the notebook down and went to sleep, crushed together in the single bed, arms, and legs flung over each other.

As the first rays of sunlight came through, Ben was up and about making a breakfast of eggs and bacon. Stephanie lay there watching him.

Ben left after breakfast.

His parting words were, "I'm a lawyer. I bet you didn't know that! Stay calm, stay away from her, unless absolutely necessary. Pretend nothing has changed. If she asks, tell her, as far as you know, Ben's going ahead with the wedding. Leave the rest to me for now."

The fifth of June was the morning of the wedding. A bright clear day, with a promise of more sunshine to come over the week. Stephanie was over early at the club, checking on the arbour under which the vows would be exchanged, the seating, the flowers. The dining hall where guests would be served dinner and speeches took most of her time. She went to the kitchen six times. The food must be just right.

The last ten days had gone in a whirlwind of activity. Ben had been strangely quiet. Stephanie had not heard from him other than, "Doing well? Waiting for the big day!"

She had made her own plans. Her bags were packed. She didn't have much, anyway.

The wedding ceremony went off without too much trouble. Ben had no family or friends. Brittany's cousin Julian served as best man. When it was over, under the flowers, the guests trooped into the dining area, where a reception area, dotted with high tables, allowed them to get drinks, sample the hors d'oeuvres and mingle. There was laughter, oohs and aahs, and deep murmur of conversation. Finally, the call came to take their places for dinner.

Julian was also serving as the MC. He walked up to the lectern near the head table and tapped on the mic.

"Is this on? Yes, it is! Good evening everyone! Thank you for coming to celebrate Brittany and Ben's wedding, on their behalf, though I'm sure they'll come on to talk to you later themselves. I just wanted to say that, there's been a small change in the program. All the speeches are being held over until the dessert comes in! Which means, nothing is going to come between you and the food! So, without further ado, let's all focus on the food first. Thanks!"

There was applause and shouts of "Yay!"

There were only twenty tables of guests, with eight to a table. It was not a very large gathering. Brittany's friends from college were there, talking at the top of their voices.

"I know!" was the phrase most heard.

As the entrée plates were removed and the dessert and coffee was brought out, Julian came back to the mic to announce the speech from the bride.

It was the lady at Table 12 who was the first to push her chair back and hurry away.

"Good evening, everyone!" was Brittany's opening words. A few more people pushed their chairs back and left in the direction of the toilets.

"Thank you all so much for coming! I'm so happy to be here with you, as Ben and I start on this journey together, as husband and wife."

More people got up and left the room. Brittany was a little surprised at the loss of people for her speech. She stopped and looked around. The tables were now down to just a handful of people, and they looked uncomfortable, too.

"First of all, I'd like say…. Excuse me, I'll be back."

She gathered up her train, jumped down from the little dais and ran for the toilets. The space outside the doors to the toilets were full of guests. Some were sitting down, with an expression of pain and surprise. Some were grimacing, as they arched their backs, trying to quell the force.

Ben, his face a picture of shock and surprise, got up to see what was happening.

The stench of faeces was filling the room. Stomachs growled, farts rent the air, the corridor was now filling up with little streams of urine and faeces and crying bridesmaids and guests.

Ben turned and found himself face to face with Stephanie.

He grabbed her by the arm and marched her towards the head table, grabbing an empty wine glass along the way.

He poured out the champagne and they clinked glasses.

"You're very lucky I have a private jet standing by. You're packed, I'm assuming?"

She nodded, struck dumb by the magnitude of what she had done.

"Excellent! Glug glug on the champagne and let's get the hell out of here. She wanted something spectacular and unforgettable. My guess is she had her wish."

He held her hand and they ran out of the door, never looking back.

A Sunset and a Dream

The rays of sleepy Sol, orange and pink and shades of red, shone like a blanket of tulips seen from afar, waving ever so gently, caressed by zephyrs in the gathering dusk.

Pink tinged feathers of clouds striped the fading blue of the sky, as the momentous day began its slow descent into night.

Wally's was warm, noisy from the clink of glasses and murmured conversation. The lights were muted and the patrons sat slumped in their seats or slouched over the bar, their hands balancing the weight on their shoulders, the head bowed, the eyes staring, unseeing, into the despair at the bottom of their glasses or mugs.

The bar was alive with custom, but, Wally, himself, wasn't there. Ever since that fateful night, the last time that Jack had been at the bar, Wally had refused to show up.

Susie, her tattoos rippling across her muscles, built up through years of bodybuilding exercises, ran the bar with near ruthless efficiency. She had Mel, who was crosseyed, blonde, and no tattoos and a brain as sharp as a butcher's knife. There was also Devon, whose every scar was a long story of a fight he had won.

Eventually, I got home. The bed was soft and warm, even though the air in the bedroom was, deliberately, cool. Images flashed through my head as a I slept, unaware of the workings of my brain, as it sifted through the collection of images, feelings, thoughts, sounds and smells I had experienced sometime, somewhere, somehow through the days when I had been awake. Or, was I awake now, and had what had passed before been merely dreams, nightmares and perceived sensations that had no connection to real life?

Dreams are when the brain initiates the process of archival, sorting and filing all the experiences into neat recesses of the mind. The feeling of déjà vu is when an experience triggers the opening of a drawer of the filing cabinet and a memory card falls to the floor, oddly related to the incident at hand.

I sat up with a start.

I knew now, why Michael had examined the library, why Estrella's car had broken down and why Jack, poor Jack, had to die.

All of this could wait, because I had to sleep off the excess of bourbon I had indulged in at Wally's Bar last evening. It could wait because Jack was already dead, Estrella innocent and Michael wasn't going anywhere, anytime soon. I checked the time.

It was three in the morning.

Tomorrow, I would collect the files, collect the last few threads of evidence I needed to close the case, convince the cops and convict the criminal.

I lay back, pulled the covers over my shoulders, which were cold from the air in the bedroom, closed my eyes and gave myself up to Morpheus.

When I awoke, it was past ten. I didn't attempt to hurry. My head felt dull, like it was filled with a viscous fluid. The morning sun was slowly disappearing under layers of clouds. The light was getting steadily greyer, the air was starting to cool with the first whisper of moisture in the air.

I made some coffee and sat down at my desk as the rain finally arrived in a steady downpour. The air took on the scent of wet mud, leaves and flowers.

I went through all the files once again, willing them to show me a different outcome. I worked steadily into the afternoon, marking, tagging and arranging the data in the files into a logical sequence. I wrote steadily, compiling the story into something I could use.

The rain had stopped. There were droplets still falling off the eaves. The colour of the clouds was changing, from a dark grey to a translucent silver. Out towards the west, there were the first patches of blue. The wind had picked up. The summer air was cooler.

The Saturday afternoon remained quiet outside. I felt the urgent need to lie down. I got into bed and closed my eyes, then checked my phone.

I called Michael. His voice was bored, tired and almost angry.

"What do you want?" he growled.

"I have it."

"Oh god, no! I don't want to know! It's Saturday, for the love of Mike!"

"You have to know. You must know what I know. Estrella is your wife! You have to know."

There was silence on the line. I waited. At least, he hadn't hung up.

"Are you sure? You're not going to waste my time, are you, with another theory?"

I was patient, but insistent.

"It's no longer a theory, Michael."

I could feel him thinking through the phone.

"Four. Be at the Kingfisher Arms."

"Upton? Four. I'm leaving now."

AJESH SHARMA

I packed the files in a cardboard box and carried it out the car. I drove for about ten minutes and then turned off towards Kingsbury Ashe. I unlocked the door of the shed, which nobody knew belonged to me. I removed the eighth floorboard and pulled out the canvas package. I didn't need to open it, but I did. I had to be sure.

The Smith and Wesson was clean. I made sure it was unloaded and clicked the trigger. I took the clip from the canvas bag and loaded it. I put the canvas bag in the boot of the car, tucked away with the spare tire. The gun I placed in the inside pocket of my jacket.

I drove a little faster back towards Upton. As I drove up, I saw Michael head into the pub. He didn't look back or around.

I followed him in. The pub was dark in the corners and bright elsewhere. He was, as I expected, sitting in one of the darkest corner, his ale in front of him. I took my own glass over to him and sat down. He nodded, raising his glass briefly.

The silence was electrically charged. The resounding echoes of each wave of silence that passed between us could have been heard across the pub. The pub, too, seemed to have fallen under the spell. The occasional laugh seemed to be muffled, the murmur of voices had died down into a barely noticeable hum, in harmony with the hum of the bees that did not exist in the pub.

We finished our drinks. He heaved himself out of the seat and I noticed the bulk that seemed to have become bigger than when I had last seen him two years ago.

"I'll drive", he said, once outside the pub.

I got in and he drove off in a small scattering of scree, as he wheeled around and accelerated right onto the road.

I followed him, easing our way with the tall hedges that seemed to conceal the road from the farms, the farmers and any livestock that may have been grazing. It took us thirty minutes to get to the clearing. He heaved himself out of the car, waited for me to get out of mine. We stood there, eyeing each other in the darkened shade from the trees that surrounded us. It seemed the wind had picked up and the temperatures were starting to fall. He flicked his hands, beckoning me to follow him. He walked through trees behind the right of his car. I followed and discovered the trail that seemed to be barely there.

We hiked through the dense woods, holding hands up to ward off marauding branches. There was a small rise and as I stepped up over it, I found myself in a small glade.

He was waiting for me, his hands by his sides, his body tense. His eyes followed me as I stepped out into the evening sun.

"Where are we? It's getting dark, so can we speed things up, otherwise finding the cars again in the dark is going to be a problem", I said.

"I won't have any trouble."

His voice was rougher than I remembered, with the veneer of social courtesy stripped away. I knew he was angry, and there was fear, too, which was natural.

"Well, where is it?" he rasped.

"Where's what?"

I could see his hands clench and then open again, as he controlled himself.

"Look. Don't waste my time. You had something for me. Now hand it over."

"I could have done that in the pub, down there. Why did you choose this place for the handover?"

"I don't have time for this! Give it to me! Now!"

"Well, Michael. If by 'it' you mean evidence that will exonerate Estrella and set her free, I have something that will do just that. But I want to know, why you chose this spot to get it. Why you're acting like you don't want anyone to know there's evidence. What are you hiding? We could have done this in the pub. Or your house. Or my office. So why here? What's the secrecy about?"

He moved, quickly and his right hand came up from his side like a scythe. I was expecting it, so I took a step back and to my left. His fist warmed the air around my chin briefly as it sped past. The movement caused him to lose his balance and he fell forward.

I watched him turn and lie there, panting.

I shook my head at him and said, "I'm going to help you up. I want no more of this nonsense, you hear? I can help you, but you have to help me. Is that clear?"

His stare was baleful, his body had that defeated feel with the loss of tension and the air of resignation. His head fall back and he lay there, staring into space.

"Can I stand up?"

"There's a fallen tree there. Sit on it and catch your breath."

He heaved himself up, dusted his knees and sat down heavily on the big tree trunk that some storm had knocked over. The sun was almost gone. The darkness of night filled the forest with a whisper of malice.

"I want answers, Michael. We're going back to your house and you're going to tell me everything. Is that clear?"

I had the gun out so he could see it. We walked back to the car, and he drove, with a sullen air of desperate resignation.

UNCOMMON PIE & OTHER STORIES

We went to the library and I set up the tripod and camera. I made him sit down so he was clearly in the frame and clipped the microphone to his shirt collar.

"Now, Michael, you know it's over. I want you to start talking. Tell the camera what happened. I want you to be clear. Estrella is innocent of Jack's murder. Now start talking. Michael, I'm your only friend now. Oh, you may have plenty of others who call themselves your friends. You may also think they are your friends. But right now, none of them can help you. I want you to help me clear up why Jack had to die. You know why Jack died. I want to know what you know. Who killed him? Why? Start talking."

I turned the camera on. Michael licked his lips, looked at me with haunted ideas, and took a deep breath.

"I saw Jack. He was with Estrella."

I watched him licking his lips and gulping like a fish searching for water.

"Tell me everything you know. From the beginning. Start with your name. Start talking."

"My name is Michael Watley.

I met Estrella Alves in Lisbon, Portugal and we married five years ago. We lived in Hockney Falls. I still live there. Two years ago, my wife met Jack Stringer. Jack Stringer and Wallace Goldsmith, known as Wally, were partners who ran a bar. Continue."

"I actually met Estrella in Sintra, not Lisbon. She was wearing high heels and they have tiles everywhere. She tripped over one of those into me. We had coffee together. Then dinner. She came back to England with me. We got married six months later.

Everything was great. We went to Mykonos for our honeymoon. She didn't want to go back to Portugal. My business trips would take me away, often for about two weeks at a time. After the first couple of years, she said she didn't want to come with me anymore.

We grew distant. I will admit that I was quite upset that she didn't seem to care to be with me. About a year ago, I came back from Paris early. I found she was with a man. They were sitting in the library. He was drinking scotch. I have a room I call my library in my house. It has a desk, sitting area with couches and all my books are stored there.

She was surprised to see me and a little concerned. She introduced me to the man. His name was Jack Stringer. She said she was talking to him about investing in a restaurant. Stringer had a pub, and wanted to expand into the restaurant business. He had an option on an old house next to the pub. He had some idea of modifying it and connecting it to the pub.

I found it a little odd. Stringer left shortly after my arrival. I asked Estrella about him, and how she came to be involved with this business. Her answers, I thought, were evasive. She changed the subject every time I would bring it up.

This happened on another occasion, a few weeks later. Again, they were in the library, talking business. The venture hadn't progressed in the intervening weeks and my suspicions grew. I suspected that there was more to this than just a business meeting.

I started coming home unexpectedly. I would also fake business trips. I found them twice more in the library. Stringer was always polite and businesslike. He carried a bag with him, in which I noticed he had a laptop. Each time he had a glass of my scotch whisky beside him.

Finally, I decided to make enquiries for myself about the property. It was no longer available for sale. The owner had decided not to sell after all, about three weeks previously.

My suspicions grew.

When I saw them again in the library, I confronted them. I demanded to know why Stringer felt it necessary to drop by so often. I told them that I had made my own enquiries and found their business plan for the property was dead, as the owner was no longer wishing to sell.

Estrella flew into a violent rage. She accused me of spying, of being suspicious. I held my ground. Stringer was quiet the whole time. Eventually, he just shook his head, packed his bag and left with the words 'I'm sorry. It isn't what you think. I feel like I'm not welcome here'.

I didn't care what he felt, and anyway, he was right. He was not welcome into my house.

Estrella and I hardly spoke after this. Two weeks later, she left for Spain. She said she wanted a break from the house and she didn't want to see me for a while.

I had been thinking about how I always met them in the library. After she left, I examined the library. It faced the driveway. I found it, cameras. There were three of them. Two down at the gate to the driveway, looking each way down the road. Then I knew I was correct in my suspicions. I left the cameras where I found them and wrote to Estrella, apologising and telling her I wanted her to come back.

She came back. I talked to her about the stress of traveling, not being there for her, not having her with me. She swallowed it all.

Then I told her I had to go away for one last trip, before I handed over that part of the business to someone else. I told her I had made plans to sell out completely.

I left for the station, took a train out to Manchester, paying by credit card. I came back on the next train, taking care to pay cash. I camped out here. If you look behind me, and climb up a little you can see the driveway across the river. I saw him drive up. Stringer.

She met him at the doorway, flung her arms around him. I waited. I waited for an hour. The police car drove up, followed by an ambulance. I saw him being carried away. The coppers stayed on for a while.

I immediately left the scene and went back to Manchester, again paying cash. When I got a call from the police, it was to let me know that Estrella was in custody on the charge of murder. I came back, spoke to the police, who told me that my wife had been hosting a gentleman and had poisoned him. It was suspected that it was a case of jealous rage leading to murder. A bottle of poisoned scotch had been found in the room.

I engaged lawyers. I was there supporting her all the way to the point they locked her up for good. I made sure they understood that Estrella did it!

I poisoned the scotch! But I made sure they knew it was Estrella who did it!

Yes. She deserved it! That deceitful, adulterous bitch!"

I switched off the recorder.

"Ok. Michael. Thank you for your confession. Now we're going to save it to your computer. Where is it?"

He took me to his study. I motioned him to connect the camera and upload it. I watched as he did. He tried to shut down the computer, but I motioned him to not bother.

"Now, Michael, how much would you say your house was worth?"

"Eh? About a couple of million pounds."

"Nice. And the partnership in the business. What is it in?"

"What do you mean?"

"What does your business do, Michael? And how much is your share of the pie?"

"We sell sanitary ware to hotels, loos, sinks, taps, and bathtubs. To inns and motels, also. We make a fair amount. I draw about hundred and fifty thousand pounds a year. My share is worth another couple of million."

"Do you have a will?"

"Yes, of course."

"Who gets your stuff when you cop it?"

"Estrella. But now she's in prison so she can't....."

He struggled to sit up, staring at me, his eyes wide with disbelief.

"Your lover? Estrella.... Was your lover?"

"Yes, Michael. Estrella loved me and I was very much in love with her. Nobody knew, because we didn't want anyone to know."

"But why?"

"Because the world is what it is, and we had our reasons."

"Oh, reasons! How long have you known her? Did you know her before I met her? Oh! I get it!"

His voice sunk to a whisper, as realization dawned.

"You bastard!"

I hit him hard with the butt of the gun in my gloved hand. He slumped over the chair, unconscious. I sat him upright. I put the gun against his temple and fired. His body went limp and his head fell back. I cleaned the gun thoroughly and put the cleaned gun, in his hand, making sure the finger was on the trigger. I placed his hand so that it lay with the gun in his lap, where it may have ended after his suicide.

I left, making sure to use minimal lights to get back on the road.

AJESH SHARMA

Six months later, the sun blazed down upon the beach. There was a whiteness everywhere, except for the bright umbrellas, the dark glasses that seemed to bloom across the white sand, like spots on a Dalmatian.

I sipped my screwdriver, placed it contentedly by my side and watched Martinique frolic. Or rather, sit and laze in the afternoon sun. I made no effort to read the book that lay on my bare chest, open at page five.

Michael Watley was a long time in the past. Estrella was not. She was there in the present. Laying on the beach chair, beside me.

The sun was burning my face. It was afternoon and last night's bourbon driven delights had clearly knocked me out harder than I had thought.

I got up, washed my face and sat down at the computer. There seemed to be a story, there, still open. I got up, made some more coffee and started to read it.

"So many plot holes!" I exclaimed!

I printed it out and made notes.

1. Why was Jack visiting Estrella?
2. Why did they install cameras?
3. What about Wally and Jack's relationship and how does it jive with Estrella?
4. Who is the writer? And what is his relationship with Wally and Jack?

At this point, I stopped. My head hurt, the coffee wasn't helping. I needed a drink, pick-me-up that would stop the jackhammer in my head from trying to break open my skull. Or better, still a nap. Yeah, a nap would be good.

UNCOMMON PIE & OTHER STORIES

I lay down and slept some more.

Discovery

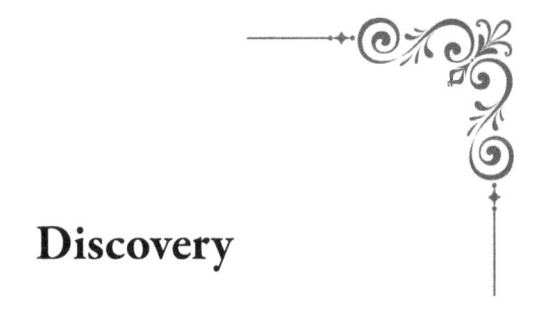

Philip Wainwright had been painting and creating art for over forty years. A trust fund baby, like the Fenworthys, he had indulged himself in a series of "arty" follies, settling on painting as his primary focus. He painted in isolation. He never displayed it and never discussed it at the social events he frequented in the evenings.

It was at one of these, that he met the tall, blond handsome James, with the tall, blonde and beautiful Rebecca by his side.

"I'm retired now. I've spent a life never having to worry about a job. Now I've turned sixty, so I tell people I'm retired and don't wish to talk about it. Saves a lot of bother", said Philip.

Rebecca said, "Oh, I know! Explaining what you did or do now is always so boring. I tell people I'm a sculptor and everyone thinks of statues, or mobiles. For some reason, I get the impression that sculpting is considered less than painting. And I work with glass, the last thing on their minds!"

"Glass is interesting. Lots of possibilities, but a lot of hard work and investment."

"And painting is not hard work?"

"Let me tell you a story", said Philip, "Once upon a time there was a painter. He was approached by a lady who wanted him to use her as the subject for his paintings and photographs. She wanted to be famous after she was gone. The artist wasn't sure if it was a good idea. She insisted and finally managed to convince him and he went ahead. In the nude, just as she wanted. She passed away shortly thereafter and the art was displayed in a glittering, crowded gallery. It was summer and the long, cold, fruity drinks flowed across the halls. The conversations centred on the art that lined the walls. The courage of the artist seemed to be the dominant theme. The courage to buck the commonly held traditions of nude portraiture and photography.

Nobody mentioned the courage of the model, the 77 year old with a double mastectomy, who was forever to remain in the photographs, her body painted in vivid colours."

"Oh! That sounds about right, sadly!" cried Rebecca.

"I see it from the point of view of the artist. It must be very difficult to the deal with the reception you get. People don't get the point of art. Most of them simply repeat what they've been told by the experts. They just don't let themselves appreciate it for themselves."

James drifted away to leave Rebecca and Philip talking about art, painting, glass and the issues with showing off art to people who either knew too much or nothing at all about art, painting or glass.

It was Rebecca's idea to host a showing of Philip's work. It took months to set up. It had taken even more to convince Philip to bring out his best or bring out anything at all.

It was James' idea to invite the Fenworthys to the showing.

The Fenworthy sisters, influential, snobbish, wealthy and devoid of empathy, wrote a column in which they reviewed the latest developments in the art world.

The column was considered one of the foremost voices in the art world. If the Fenworthys said the art was terrible, it was deemed so, and the acolytes within the idle and rich strata avoided it. If they said it was great, the community nodded in assent and scuttled away to relay the message among their acquaintances. Some of them even acquired the masterpiece.

Justine Fenworthy was sixty two, had been rumored to have had numerous lovers in her lifetime, not one of whom had ever been seen by anyone. Her older sister, Nadine, was sixty five and a seeming champion of celibacy as a personality trait.

So when Philip Wainwright's art collection finally went on display, the social circles waited to hear from the two sisters what they should say and how they should perceive his work.

Rebecca was at the Summer Art Festival when Susie brought her the paper, folded to show the Fenworthy review. The gasps reverberated through her head in a crescendo of sound. The crash of the falling piece as she pushed it over, accompanied by the cries of the viewers in the gallery was, however, a silent one. She could see it, but not hear it. She could feel her feet stamping, her hands clenched, the screaming from her throat, but it seemed like she was in a soundproof cell.

At that point, she hated everyone; the Fenworthy sisters, for their sadistic reviews, the people who ate up their every word without thinking for themselves and, most of all, James, for inviting the sisters to review Philip's work.

She left the gallery, her latest creation lying in broken pieces of glass on the floor.

Two weeks later, she moved into the remote cottage by the beach where she spent her first few days engulfed in tears that flowed down her cheeks to match the rain that came and went at regular intervals outside the window.

The rain bothered her. It had been raining, it seemed, ever since she had arrived, three months ago. It felt like she'd lived here forever and the rain had poured down forever. It had been raining all night and now at 8AM, it came down in a steady downpour

The cottage sat on the edge of the beach. The deck, always wet, had been sold as the perfect place to sit, gazing at the ever changing patterns of the waves crashing and heaving upon the beach, about 50 meters away. She'd tried to sit there, the rain pouring down on her head, washing away the minimal makeup together with the tears that rolled down her cheeks.

That was the last time she had cried, sitting there in the rain, the waves racing up and throwing themselves on the shore, the wind whipping her hair around her face like wet whiplashes. She'd needed those two hours to work it out of her system.

The tears were gone, but the thoughts remained. They would never go. She didn't want them to. She wanted to remember the days. She just didn't want the memory of them to hurt her anymore. She also knew there would always be hurt, hopefully numbed and in the background.

The walls of the room inside were white painted board, hung with the watercolours she had painted so often in her teenage years and her early twenties. The sofa had more throw cushions than any average person would want in a lifetime. She had seemingly collected cushions without let or hindrance. Or remorse. She may have had some remorse for some of the things she had done, but absolutely none for buying cushions. They appealed to her, in every conceivable colour or pattern, or texture.

Robin had once commented, "It's a replacement for the glass sculptures you refuse to produce".

Maybe, Robin had been right about that. But she could not, would not go back to glass; not after that fiasco.

Rebecca picked up her cup, settled back and pulled the blanket closer around her. She drank her coffee, the mug cupped in both hands. Her phone buzzed. She ignored it. It buzzed again. She picked it up and saw it was Susie. A text message followed.

'Coming around. Be there in 15 minutes. Get the coffee started. Or wine...'

She sat on the porch. The wind had died and the rain had eased into a barely perceptible drizzle. Just around 11 AM, a car drove up, with Robin at the wheel. Susie jumped out, waving frantically from the passenger seat. She came running up to the porch and flung herself at Rebecca.

Behind her came Robin, followed by him, James Dodd, tech millionaire, art aficionado, and ex husband. Susie saw Rebecca stiffen and cried out.

"Oh Becky! We had to get James here. Robin and I are dead tired of watching him crying copiously all day, everyday!"

"Oh yeah! What's his problem? James, what's eating you now?"

James stood there, hands in the pockets of his slacks. There was an awkward silence, before he spoke.

"The memory of what we had. It won't go away. I wanted to see you and tell you that. But these guys wouldn't tell me where to find you. And nobody else seemed to know also."

"Well, you've told me that, and now you know where I am."

Rebecca's trembling lip betrayed her defiance.

"Robin and Susie, why did you tell him and why did you bring him?" she asked.

Susie said, "Oh, Becky! I couldn't take it anymore. The thought of you mooning around here and him mooning around over there was driving me crazy and, darling, it's time."

"Is it, Rebecca? Is it time? Is it time to add to those memories we can't forget?" said James.

Rebecca turned to the window. The rain had stopped, the day had brightened. Out across the sea she could see shafts of sunlight streaking down to the water.

"We can have lunch", she said.

Robin said, "I got a picnic hamper in the car."

They took the chairs down to the beach and ate sandwiches, and fruit, washed down with wine.

Robin said, "Oh, did you know that Philip Wainwright has disappeared."

"I haven't read the news in months", Rebecca replied, "Is he really gone?"

"Yes. He was never quite the same after that review of his work. The Fenworthys had taken, it seemed, a special dislike to the Wainwright collection. He was last seen getting into cab, with a backpack and small suitcase. The art gallery had reached out to him without any success. Eventually his paintings were taken down and stored away."

Rebecca didn't feel she could say anything about this piece of news.

In the afternoon, she watched them walk back to the car. Robin and Susie settled in. James, stood there, his hand on the door. He waved at her, a small gesture, almost not a gesture at all. Then he ducked into the back seat. Robin turned the car around, waved at her and they drove off.

UNCOMMON PIE & OTHER STORIES

Once they were safely out of sight, Rebecca set to work packing up. She took a backpack, shut down the cottage, making sure it was secured, then called a cab and took a train into London.

Raising Tim, Jeff and Margorie required many phone calls, many explanations and many meetings. Four months later in the village of Whitstone, the four of them sat in the quiet pub, talking in hushed tones. There were just the four of them and a handful of locals in the pub. Outside the moon had just appeared in a cloudless sky.

Rebecca's voice was urgent and passionate.

"It has to be. I'm sure of it! There's no other place he could be. I'm not sure why it's taken so long for you to understand that!"

"Yes, Rebecca, I am inclined to agree with you. But we couldn't just go rushing off on a mere whim. Hold on! I wasn't going to say your theory is a whim. As I said, I also think this is most likely. Anyway, we're here and we'll go tomorrow and check it out", said Jeff.

"Don't you see? Philip Wainwright has to be there. You guys don't know him as I do. When he disappeared, two years ago, everyone assumed he'd gone away to the Bahamas. And, to be fair, those initial postcards from him were quite suggestive. But then, Noddy Sewell went to the Bahamas and couldn't find him. Nobody seemed to know him, or of him. And his disappearance was written off as just another artist deciding to retire somewhere out of sight."

Tim said, "Well, we'll test out the hypothesis tomorrow. Anyone want another round?"

Nobody wanted another. They finished the last of their respective drinks, walked out of the pub to the little inn, a quarter mile away, and retired to their rooms.

They arrived in the little hamlet of Hexworthy just after 11 AM the next morning. They parked the car on the main street and looked around them. Margorie spread her iPad out on the bonnet of the car and they all peered at it. There was just one hill, which wasn't too high, but which didn't seem to have a path leading up to what looked like a shepherd's hut at the top.

"It has to be. Come on, let's check it out, doesn't look like it's too hard", said Jeffrey.

They shrugged into their backpacks and set off. Very quickly, it became apparent that despite not being very high, the walk up was not going to be easy. The stony hillside was overgrown with bushes and there was no discernible path. Ninety minutes later, they arrived at the stone cottage.

The sunlight streamed through in violent, dusty motes. Dust lay everywhere. Every piece of furniture, not covered in dusty tattered sheets, contained a thick layer of dust. There was no sign of violence in the room. It was simply a room, dust laden, quiet, lit up by sunlight, devoid of any signs of life. Human life, that is.

They entered the cottage in silence. The air of gloom, dust and despair filled their hearts with foreboding. Decay was the essence of the room. It smelled foul, like a mixture of decay, of paint, of turpentine, of alcohol and human flesh might be expected to smell.

The four walked around the room, examining the paintings on the wall. Tim, walked over to a couple of easels and removed the sheets.

The four of them stared at the two portraits. The canvas on which they were painted, glowed with a violent light. The silence of the room was replaced, it seemed, by an earth shattering roar, as they stood there in silence.

Justine Fenworthy lay, half on her back, naked on a bed, one hand posed seductively behind her head. In the other portrait, Nadine Fenworthy, her sister, stood by a fireplace, facing the viewer, one hand on her naked hip, the other lying limply by her side.

Rebecca walked into the next room and let out a scream. She rushed out, and out of the cottage, sobbing hysterically.

Jeff went into the room to see what had cause Rebecca to rush out like that. The dead body lay where it had fallen. Philip Wainwright had been dead a long time in that dusty room.

The newspapers, tabloids and TV screens lit up with the sensational news.

"Artist Philip Wainwright found dead. Stunning nude portraits of Justine and Nadine Fenworthy, noted art critics, found in previously unseen collection of Wainwright canvases, together with other nude portraits. The Fenworthys have declined to comment."

Rebecca checked into her London apartment, and called James. They met at his narrowboat in the Regents Canal.

The conversation was stilted. The bottle of Chianti was emptied and James got up to get another.

"Cabernet, I'm afraid. Let me see how you like this one."

He picked up the corkscrew and expertly popped the cork.

"I'll just let it breathe for a couple of minutes."

Rebecca picked up her glass and said, "Can I get a glass of water, please? I just need to wash the taste of the Chianti first, if you don't mind."

"Sure. Let me get you one."

He ducked down into the boat. Rebecca watched him and quickly emptied the contents of the little bottle she took from her bag into the bottle of wine. She had replaced the bottle and was standing by the rail when James returned with a glass of water.

"You know, it's really great to see you again. I thought you had completely given up on me. Even if it's just a truce, I'll drink to it."

He poured out the wine and raised his glass in a silent toast to her.

"This moment deserves a healthy draught!"

He took a mouthful, swirled it around and grimaced, before swallowing.

"Ouch, tastes foul. I think it's gone bad. Are you sure you're ok?"

"Oh yes. This is just fine for me".

"You haven't tasted it yet", he said slowly, realization dawning.

She took the glass out of his hand and watched him sink to the floor in slow motion.

It took four weeks to properly catalogue and safely transport all the paintings. It took just two more to set up the show.

The announcement of The Philip Wainwright Collection took pains to reiterate that the artist had been found dead in a remote cottage by a group of his most devoted fans, who were working on a hunch, and his collection included stunning new art that was guaranteed to shake up the art world, and society as a whole would never be the same again.

Just next to it, was a smaller section with the headline.

More than a month has gone by since noted art patron, James Dobb, was reported missing. His ex wife has no knowledge of his whereabouts. His narrowboat was found adrift fifteen miles from its usual mooring. Nobody was onboard.

The Philip Wainwright show was met with mixed reactions. Consternation, confusion, anger and shame ran through the socialite circles. Amusement, derision and a certain degree of smugness enveloped the rest of the viewers. TV shows, newspaper articles and magazines analyzed the effect of the collection in glee.

Rebecca could not be reached for comment, on the art collection and the disappearance of her ex-husband. She had left town to drive through the remote countryside, stopping at little villages, finding small inns. She desperately needed to be away from everyone, anyone who knew her.

Driving into the countryside, she had no thought about what she might find. The discovery of the little villages, the trails and the countryside had, at first, saddened her. She felt the loneliness and isolation would be a burden on the residents of the villages.

What she discovered was vibrant communities, cheerful people that sat in the small pubs, sometimes the only one in the town. There was talk, there were voices, conversation. The journey had been conceived as an escape. It had turned into a voyage of learning and discovery. She was left questioning her life as an artist, manufacturing pieces of glass for the pleasure of an audience that couldn't appreciate what it meant to produce the work. Oftentimes, catering to what would, presumably, sell against what she wanted to produce.

The five kilometre hike she was on felt tougher than it had seemed to be from the village. Rebecca slogged through the uphill trail. Her head was still not fully clear of the anger, fear and doubt that she had felt since she had left, run away, from the city.

She arrived at the top of the hill where the ruins of the castle that had probably once been the seat of local power centuries ago lay in the early afternoon sun. The roofs were gone, some of the walls, too. Plant life, only too happy to take over, had done just that. Down below she could see the village. The trail was barely visible.

Rebecca stood at the threshold, scanning the room for any sign of life, past or present. There was none. Other than the dust, the cobwebs in the corners, the soot of a thousand fires that had once burned constantly, there was nothing to see.

The walls were bare of any decoration. There was no furniture, no artifacts, no remnant of a past time. There were windows in one wall that looked west and the sun was beginning to come through, creating a thin rectangle of light on the bare, dusty floor.

Rebecca shrugged her backpack off her shoulders, laid it on the floor and slumped against the wall. She bit another bite off her granola bar and gave herself up to a moment of nothingness, blanking her mind, trying to shake free of the sadness and guilt.

She sat there as the rectangle of light grew on the floor at her feet. When it reached her boot, she knew it was time to go. It was downhill, but would still take more than an hour back to the hamlet at the base of the hill.

She heaved the backpack on and turned at the threshold for one final look at the only room in the ruins that was still standing with a roof. The rest of the castle had long ago fallen into itself.

Time, it was said, erased everything. Indeed, the castle had all but been erased. The room, stood defiant, for now. In time, it, too, would be erased.

Maybe, some time in the future, perhaps, someone would come up the hill and make their own discovery of the signed confession that she had left behind in the far corner of that bare room.

Back at her seaside cottage, Rebecca sat on the beach, the waves lapping gently at her feet, her glass of wine in her hand, her sunglasses keeping out the sun that beat down upon her.

The Plan

It's not every day that a man learns that his wife is in a sexual relationship with another woman.

In the car, therefore, he was unusually silent. Smita knew that if Sushil Deka was silent, then the situation was serious. She had expected that. She did not break the silence as she concentrated on threading her way through the city traffic. Once they were on the highway to the airport, she felt the time had come to talk.

"I'm sorry, Sushil. I didn't want to break it to you like this."

He stared ahead and said nothing.

"So, wanna talk about it?" Smita asked.

"Smita, there isn't much to talk about, is there? I need time to process the situation. I can't respond to it until then."

"You really believe that? You're not normally this slow at coming to a decision. Aren't you even going to try?"

"I ...," he broke off, shaking his head and staring out at the road ahead. Smita kept just below the speed limit. She needed all her concentration for this conversation.

"You, what? Go ahead, let's hear it."

She wanted to push him into reacting, into screaming out loud.

"Look, Smita, here's the thing. I need to go away for a bit. You have issues. I have issues. You've known me a long time. I'm not someone given to kneejerk reactions. In fact, you yourself have said, many times, that you wished I was more impulsive."

"Spontaneous, not impulsive," Smita wanted to make that clear.

She was treading on thin ice here. Sushil had a temper that flared suddenly. He did not respond, which was a good thing. Or was it? Out of the corner of her eye, she got the impression of a sudden straightening of his body. She risked a quick glance over and he was rigid in the seat, the seatbelt seemed to cut him in half. Maybe it was just her imagination.

"Maybe if you opened your mind and looked at it from my point of view it will help. You've been away so often for so long. I'm not sure how it happened. Let's be honest. It wasn't a nice thing to do to you. I should have spoken to you earlier about it. I shouldn't have let it happen. Maybe, I felt a lack of companionship and let it get the better of me, cloud my judgement."

"Did she talk you into it? I can't quite understand how it happened. She must have pushed you into it."

"What you really want to know is if I'm in love with her."

"Maybe. I don't know. I just don't want you hurt. Is she nice to you?"

For a minute, he was silent, his hand moved as if he was trying to say something, but couldn't. Finally, he got it out.

"You know, whatever happens, happens for a reason. I didn't choose to be away. It was a matter of work. I wasn't to know it would take so much from our relationship. It was an insidious thing."

"It just crept up on you, did it?"

"Yes"

"Oh, so now you know how it happened to me."

"You are going to equate work with a same-sex relationship?"

"No, I'm talking about the way life overtakes us. Has overtaken us."

"I think there is a difference, though."

At least she had him talking. She'd been afraid that the ride to the airport was going to be a long and painfully quiet one, full of bruised egos, regret and guilt.

"How is it any different? You developed a relationship with work, didn't you? And it took you over and took you away from me. You didn't mean that to happen. Or did you?"

The memory of the lonely nights waiting for Sushil to come back from his trips came flooding back to Smita.

"You're clever", he said.

She glanced over. He was looking at her.

"Not clever enough to not let that happen to me, too."

"I had already got the point you were trying to make", he snapped back.

"What is the point I was trying to make?"

"That you did not mean to. It just happened."

His voice was mocking, his head nodding with the effort. Smita waited. She didn't want to say it, so she waited for him to say it.

"The fact is, nothing happens to us that we don't allow to happen to us."

It was out there, finally.

"So you admit that you preferred work over me?"

"Just like you admit that you preferred the company of another woman to mine."

"Are we calling it quits then?"

She wanted to know. She suddenly realized that she wanted to know quite desperately.

"That's what we have to figure out."

"Is that why you are going away? Or is it work related?"

"My going away today was work related."

The inflection on the "was" and the past tense caught her off guard.

"Was?"

"Yes, it was scheduled. You may or may not be surprised to hear that I have cancelled all my meetings for the week. Personal health reasons."

"So you're going to Hyderabad, but not going to work?"

"Who said I'm going to Hyderabad? I told you. I cancelled all my sessions."

"So where are you going?"

"I'm just going to disappear for a while. Lie around and think. Today is Monday. I shall get myself off the grid till the end of the week for sure. Then we shall see."

She wanted to ask. She wanted to know. Somehow, she did not want him to go away and not be able to connect with him. A wave of sudden nausea swept over her.

"Watch it!"

She got the car back under control.

"Sorry."

They drove on in silence. Smita could sense him looking at her with care. It made her feel good. She couldn't explain it, but it did. They were approaching the airport now and as she turned off the ramp, he spoke again.

"Drop me curbside. Terminal 1."

She whipped a look at him.

"No. I'm coming in."

He didn't say anything. Smita focused on negotiating the lane mergers that always annoyed her about airports and then headed towards long term parking. She ignored his protestations about curbside drop offs. She wasn't just going to see him off at the curb. He took his bag out of the car and she saw now that it was a big bag, not the carryon he normally took for his trips. He slung his laptop bag over his shoulder and wheeled his suitcase along as they walked into the terminal.

"You want to find out where I'm going, don't you?"

He sounded slightly amused, she felt, by that.

"Yes. I don't like the fact that you are going to bury yourself away somewhere and not be able to talk. I don't like the idea of you cutting off all communication."

They walked up to the Lufthansa counter and checked his bag in. He was on the flight to Munich.

Munich! Why Munich? Thoughts, questions and wild accusations welled up inside her. Why Munich?

"You have plenty of time before your flight," she said, as he turned away from check in.

"Coffee?"

"Sure."

They took their coffees over to the uncomfortable airport seats and sat down in silence.

"So Munich, huh?"

"Yes."

"You're wondering why Munich, aren't you?"

"I am, yes."

"Well, let me put your mind at ease. I don't have a second wife there."

"That wasn't what I meant and you know it."

"That's exactly what you meant and you know it," he said, with a trace of temper.

She didn't, couldn't, say anything. He broke the silence.

"Look, I have to think. This flight will take me to Munich. Then I'll figure out what next."

"You always have a plan. You're telling me you're going to go to Munich and you don't have a plan?"

"Yes," he said in a curiously tight voice.

Smita leaned over and looked up at him.

"Look, if it means anything, I'm sorry it turned out this way."

They sat there in silence as the minutes ticked away. Then it was time for him to go through the security check in. They walked with what seemed like slow steps up to the big sliding glass door. He turned and gave her a quick hug.

"Thanks for driving me here. I'll be getting along now. You drive back safely, okay?"

"Bye", is all she could manage.

He strode away. She watched him as he walked up to the door. This was it; she could almost sense the time running out like sand through her fingers. Somewhere in the recesses of her brain, a countdown began.

Ten, nine, eight, seven, six, five...

She got down to "two" before he stopped and turned. His face a study in self control, he walked back, with decisive steps. He slipped the bag off his shoulder and let it rest at his feet. She saw as much as felt his left hand on her shoulder, squeezing very gently.

"I have to go now."

She felt the accent on the 'have'. She said nothing. She waited. He searched her face for an eternity. She felt nothing, her body felt hollow; a hollowness that was surprisingly heavy.

A voice said, "Take care of yourself."

With surprise she realized, it was hers. She'd been sure that the shell that was her body had neither a brain nor muscles to process thought, let alone convert it into speech. His hand squeezed a little tighter, then he slung his bag over his shoulder again, looking into her face again as if searching for something.

He walked away as decisively as he had walked towards her. The sliding frosted glass door opened and swallowed him. She stood there for a brief moment, wondering how she should feel, how she did feel. Then she, too, turned away and walked back to the car, got in and drove back home. She turned the key in the lock, walked in, turned the TV on and stared at it.

When the doorbell rang, it was Sheena; Sheena, her lover, the other woman in Sushil's life, eight years younger than Smita, with lovely hair, flashing eyes and hungry lips.

"Hi, I tried calling your cell and got no answer."

"I went to the airport to drop him off. I didn't want to be disturbed."

"Oh. How did it go? I'm sorry for putting you through it. I wish I'd been there."

Smita wasn't sure that would have been a good thing, but she didn't say so. She sat down in front of the TV again. Sheena, she could see, wanted to talk. Smita didn't.

"He's gone away for a few days. To think, he says. He's on a flight to Munich."

Sheena nodded. There didn't seem much to say so they sat and watched the TV in silence. From the corner of her eye, Smita watched Sheena. She'd have to give her up. He was lost forever. She was going to lose them both. Her mind whirled through the possibilities, unable to fix on anyone with any certainty. Sheena, always perceptive, knew better than to open a conversation.

The day wore on, uneasily, broken by the usual business of preparing dinner. Some semblance of conversation returned as they ate. Sheena recounted another anecdote from her work; a fairly amusing little tale of a mix-up and the near catastrophic loss of a client's eyebrows. Some of the stories she told Smita were, Smita suspected, more than a little embellished. Sheena had given up her career in advertising to take over the management of the spa her family owned. Embarrassing encounters and crises seemed to occur daily according to her.

They went to bed early. Smita flicked on the TV in the bedroom to watch the news. The usual collection of mayhem, murder and political chaos flashed by in a blur on the very busy screen. Reporters yelled out the news, an endless loop of video ran in the top right corner and a ticker tape scrolled by at breakneck speed at the bottom. Just above that, the weather kept changing from a week's supply of clouds and sun to an hourly forecast. She turned to look at Sheena. She was lying on her back, looking at Smita.

Smita flipped the TV off, put the remote away and turned off the light. She slid under the covers and in the darkness, Sheena moved over to put her arms around Smita. She knew better than to make any advances and they lay there for a while.

When they woke, it was because of the light that was flooding the room from the blinds they had forgotten to draw shut the night before. Smita padded over to the kitchen to put some coffee on. She could hear Sheena in the bathroom. As Smita finished setting up the coffee percolator, she came in.

"I'll put some toast on. You've brushed your teeth?"

"No. I wanted to get the coffee started first. You look after it; I'll be back in a couple of minutes."

They sat at the table next to the open French windows, sipping coffee. She'd lathered the toast with marmalade. She looked at Smita as she munched away.

"You like a lot of marmalade on your toast," she said.

"Yep. Nothing beats marmalade on toast; especially with a cup of coffee."

"Well, I took the day off today. I know you did too. So what's the plan for the day?"

"I don't quite know. I just knew that I'd like a day off...," Smita tailed off.

She nodded.

"Well, let's just finish breakfast and play it by ear. I'm going to take a shower. Maybe, we should go out and get some lunch and talk."

"Yes. It is a pity."

"Is it? We can't all live in this triangle forever! You're going to choose?"

"I don't know. I barely had my coffee! Get off my back. Go take a shower or something. We'll figure something out."

"You know, the thing that really confuses me is how he just left. You said he didn't have a plan. He was just going to chill? Really? That doesn't sound right."

"Yes. That bothers me too. He always has a plan."

"Well. I'm going to take a long bath."

Smita watched her body under the almost sheer, knee high nightie as she walked away. She felt, again, the nausea, as she thought of Sushil, of Sheena, of the choice she would have to make. She sat there for what seemed a long time, waiting for the feeling of dread to fade away. She heard Sheena's hair dryer go for a while. Then she came in, dressed in a pale pink silk blouse tucked into a pair of tight jeans.

"Go take a shower, I'll put the breakfast stuff away."

Lunch at the new Italian restaurant was interesting in the food and boring in the conversation. In keeping with the mood of the day, they engaged in odd bits of conversation, with no topic seemingly getting off the ground.

Smita said, "I don't know what induced me to have that pesto spaghetti. It lacked flavor. Do you think they were very offended when I asked for some hot sauce?"

"You should have got the garlic shrimp on the side. You said you were going to get that and then you changed your mind. You do that a lot you know. You say you want something as you read the menu, and then when the time comes to order you pick something different."

"Why does that bother you?"

"It's a little annoying, especially so, because later on, you'll complain about whatever it was you actually did order. So why not order what you said you liked in the first place?"

"I can change my mind, can't I? There's no law against it, is there?"

"No. There isn't. Why do you do it? Somewhere in the back of your head must be a reason."

"There's no dark secret! Why are you being so rude?"

"OK! Have it your way! Next time, we go out, change your mind three or four times. Whatever!"

"I'm going in there. I want to buy a scarf."

They came back toting a bag of shoes, two blouses and no scarf.

Smita flung the packages aside and disappeared into the bedroom. She appeared with "The Valley of Fear" and flopped onto the sofa, stretching out full length after adjusting the cushions.

"Sherlock again? Haven't you read that like a million times already?"

"I like to re-read. It relaxes me and you're not being very nice to me today. Especially, when..." she stopped and opened her book.

"Especially? Why? Because Sushil's abandoned you without telling you what he's up to? You want to know everything and he's deliberately left you out."

"How dare he just... just... just go away, just like that?"

"Ah. You wanted a scene and he deprived you of your big scene, eh?"

"I think you're being absolutely horrid to me today. I'm going to read. You can do whatever. Just don't talk to me."

She read, furiously turning pages, before settling down into a steady state. Sheena pulled out her phone and played a few games.

Smita was still reading when Sheena assembled a salad for herself. Eventually, Smita put her book aside and made a lightly sautéed rice and vegetable mash for herself. They ate separately, the TV ran a game show. Neither of them paid much attention to it.

The next day, Sheena left for the spa. Smita busied herself in putting away the breakfast dishes, and doing some desultory dusting. This became the pattern for the next few days.

It was Sunday morning when Smita found the long envelope in the mail. It had a foreign postmark on it, in German. She ripped it open and found a printout of a confirmation email from Swissair to Mr. Sushil Deka. It listed the itinerary for two passengers for the flight to Zurich on Monday, for Mrs. Smita Deka and Miss Sheena Singh.

There was a note from him.

'I'll pick you up at Zurich airport. We can spend some time in Switzerland and then head out to Austria. There's this lovely little hotel in Salzburg and there's always Mozart in the air. See you... with or without. Sushil.'

A wave of emotion swept over her. She recognized anger, quickly followed by relief. She ran over and hugged Sheena.

Sheena said, "What are you so happy about?"

"It's him!"

"What's he saying?"

"He's sent two tickets."

"Tickets? For what?"

"Airline tickets. Flight to Zurich."

"What?"

"He says he can pick us up at the airport and drive us to Salzburg, Austria."

"Well, he's being a little presumptuous, isn't he?"

"Is he? Is he, really?"

She gazed at Smita for a few seconds.

"You want me to make the decision for you."

Smita scanned her face anxiously.

"I'm not going to. You need to figure out what's important to you. It's you who has to decide", she said.

They argued all evening. Smita pleaded and threatened alternately. Sheena withstood the onslaught.

She walked away and flopped on the couch, her back to Smita. Smita stood there, alone in a welter of emotions, the warmth of the sunshine streaming through the window doing nothing to take away the ice that was flowing through her veins.

Eventually, she walked away to the shower. When she came out, Sheena was still sitting there.

"We're not doing our Saturday lunch. It's off." she said with a note of finality.

"Why? Where are you going?"

"You need to figure out what you want to do."

"I don't want you to go", Smita cried.

"Listen, Smita, you need to make up your mind. I don't believe you're committed one way or the other. This can't go on, not like this."

"But we're so good for each other!"

"Well, my dear, I'm sorry. You need to sort your head out."

They stared at each other. Sheena got up and headed out for the bedroom. When she came out, Smita saw the small overnight bag she carried was in her hand.

Sheena stopped at the door and looked back at Smita, a brief fleeting glance of pity, before she pulled the door open and left.

Once Smita had finished crying, she sat down to pack. She fussed over what to carry and what to leave behind. Finally, she packed just a carryon.

"He can buy me new stuff and I'll get a bag there! He owes me!"

Monday at the airport, Smita wheeled her bag along and had a co-passenger lift it on the overhead bin. She settled down for the flight to Zurich. The flight was uneventful. She settled down and watched a detective movie that left her unsatisfied. The coincidences that led to the deduction were just too many.

At Zurich, she hurried out and broke into a half run as she spotted Sushil.

"You're so bad! I knew you had a plan!"

"You keep saying I always have a plan!"

"You do! You never do anything impulsive."

"Well, never mind. I guess Sheena didn't want to come?"

Smita's face clouded. She shook her head.

Sushil took her bag and waved her on. They walked way to the car.

"It's early still. The nice thing about these flights is that they arrive in the morning so you get a day's worth in almost."

"So what do we do today? Check into the hotel first?"

"No. Let's go for a drive. It's a lovely day. I have a surprise."

"Ah! A plan!"

"You know you're a Sherlock Holmes freak, right?"

"Oh my god! No!"

"Yep!"

As they arrived at Reichenbach Falls, Smita was excited enough to actually skip.

"Hike first! Please Sushil, I want to see the scene of the fight where Moriarty fell to his death."

It was just past Bergstation, the part of the hike over the falls, when Smita, peering over the edge, lost her footing and fell headlong into the depths below.

Her shriek was cut short on the way down as her heart gave way from fright. He looked around at the trail ahead and behind him. He could see no one. He had made sure of that before the accident.

He turned and walked back down to Bergstation and road the funicular back to the car and drove off.

Three weeks later, Sushil Deka unlocked the door to his apartment and picked up the junk mail outside his door. As he peered at the contents, the elevator opened and his neighbour across the hall stepped out.

"Hello. You are back from business trip? I have not seen your wife for some time. She also went with you?"

"No. She's at home."

"Oh no, sir, I saw her leave with her bag, about, uh, two or three weeks ago."

"What? That's odd. Ok, thanks! I'll go and check. Maybe, someone in the family had a medical emergency. Her uncle wasn't well, I know."

"She had a friend who would come over often. I haven't seen her in a while."

The tone was inquiring, meaning to be friendly, but containing a fair amount of curiosity.

"Ah, yes, they were once neighbours back in the day. They grew up together. Smita is like an elder sister to her."

He went through the apartment. He found the letter that he had sent from Munich. He took the letter and the envelope, tore them into little pieces. He put them into the pan with the vented glass lid. He poured a little bit of lighter fluid and lit the paper, shutting the lid immediately to control the smoke. The ashes he flushed down the drain.

He made phones calls to Smita's uncle and created the tension he needed. Most of their few friends and acquaintances had heard nothing as well. He waited till 9 PM before heading to the police station as a distraught husband to file a missing person report. The week went by. There was no trace of Smita. She was last seen leaving the building carrying a bag. After that, there was no trace of her.

As the months went by, the neighbors no longer avoided his eye. Faint traces of pity tinged their faces when they ran into him. Sushil ensured they felt his sorrow, so they could understand when he put the apartment up for sale and moved out of the city.

It took another six months before they felt it safe enough for Sheena to join him.

QT and The East

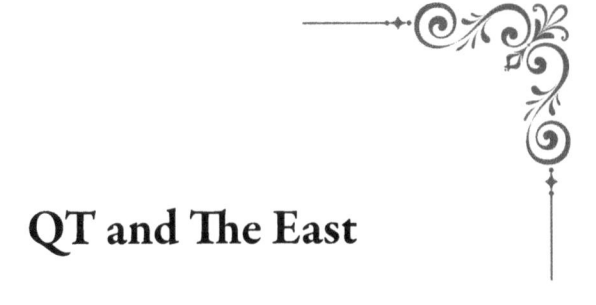

Ryan East walked across from his house to his bakery next door. It was 5 AM. This was his normal routine.

Ryan was sixty five years old. He had moved here five years ago, retiring from nearly forty years of life in the insurance industry, where he had used his exceptional mathematical skills to carve out a name for himself as an actuary and a skilled practitioner in the art and science of evaluating risk.

His retirement was a subdued affair. Most people treated him with awe, and he had developed a manner that invited a sort of reverence. When asked what he planned to do in retirement, he answered with the sort of clarity people expected from him.

"I've got an option on this bakery, about an hour away. Quiet place, a gentle stream next door. I shall start baking."

Most people agreed that the sort of relaxed precision required in the baking process would suit Ryan just fine.

It worked as expected. Ryan had rejuvenated the bakery. The freshly painted sign said, "The East – artisanal bakery". The East specialized in sourdough based breads and other baked good and generated a healthy income. Ryan didn't care about the income. Judicious investments and a life of high paying jobs ensured funds were sufficient, bordering on munificient.

He was happy calculating the precise measure of water, salt and flour to match the yeast to make his experiments work.

He experimented everyday. From four to six every morning, he busied himself with baking stuff for the paying public. In the afternoon, he experimented for himself, carefully measuring ingredients and making notes. The successes duly appeared in the store. The failures were met with pursed lips. The sheet of paper with numbers and remarks were filed neatly for future use, in a file titled "Doesn't Work". This file sat against the file of successes. This was titled "Works". There was also a file that mapped out cost and pricing details. This file was titled "Dollars and Sense".

A very neat, methodical approach, it was and no one who had known Ryan East in his career would have been surprised by it all.

With the morning's baking out into the shelves, Ryan turned on the soft lights in the shop and made sure that all the shelves were arranged properly to show off the goods. He then pulled the window shades up, flipped the "Closed" sign to "Open" and unlocked the front door, precisely at 7 AM.

He smoothed his apron, and was about to head back behind the counter, when he saw a car pull up across the street.

For a moment, nobody got out, so Ryan had a chance to inspect the low slung Mercedes roadster. He had never been interested in one, preferring the solid efficiency of the E Class. Living next door to the bakery, and busy with the shop till late afternoon, he didn't need one. Anyway, driving through the country roads needed something more robust and his Land Rover served him much better.

He was just about to go back inside, when the door opened and a lady stepped out. She was tall, with long legs encased in tight jeans, her blonde, curly hair cascading down over the shoulders of her brilliant red blouse. She paid no attention to Ryan, locked the car, and walked up to the door across from Ryan's bakery. He watched her unlock the door and head inside.

"Good morning, Mr. East", said the voice behind him.

He turned to see the gaunt and wizened face of Eva Gardner. She was, so the saying went in town, ageless. Nobody could recall a time when Mrs. Gardner had not appeared promptly at seven in the morning, dressed and ready to strike up a conversation with anyone. Those who considered themselves fortunate to meet her were usually artists of some kind, writers, painters, dramatists who could get an enormous quantity of ideas from her monologues.

The unfortunate ones were those who were in a hurry to get somewhere. Ryan was neither. He liked chatting with her in the morning, because she was the only one there. The rest of the shoppers didn't usually appear until almost eight.

"Ah, good morning, Mrs. Gardner! It's a beautiful day we're getting today, it looks like."

"Well, you know, it's never a good thing to be too optimistic. You must balance optimism with a bit of pessimism and lots of realism. I have found that to be a very healthy way of avoiding disappointment."

"I fully agree! You know, I built a career out of it."

"Yes. Actuary, you were. I wonder why they didn't call it being an 'actually'. That's what you people did. Take everything you see and hear and build out an actuality out of it."

"Now, Mrs. Gardner, that is an excellent way to look at it! They should have put you in charge!"

"The house was sold two weeks ago, you know."

"The one across there?"

"Yes. I saw you looking at it. The lady is going to be trouble for us."

"Well, come, come, we don't know her."

"Her clothes are too tightfitting, you see. She will be trouble."

"Well, we'll see. Now, what can I pack up for you today?"

Ryan was behind the counter, ready for Mrs. Gardner, when she suddenly seemed to clutch at the counter, her eyes turning inward. Ryan hurried around and got to her just as she fell. He laid her gently to the floor. She seemed to have fainted. Ryan reached for the telephone and the ambulance arrived to certify that old Mrs. Gardner was beyond saving.

Through the fuss and the small crowd that had gathered, Ryan became aware of a flash of red. He looked up to see the new neighbour, stand back as the old lady's body was removed from the bakery.

The few people who had come to sniffle at the passing of the old lady, had left, when Ryan found himself alone with the lady in red.

"Hello. Sorry to see that on my first day here. How old was she?"

"Hi. Nobody knows. She seemed to have been here forever. She was a regular visitor. Often came just to chat. I liked that."

"Hmm. It's actually good she passed without any long lingering health issues. I'd like to go like that, too. Suddenly, without warning. Poof! And I'm gone."

Ryan nodded, unable to react to the light manner in which the lady had dismissed the death.

"Of course, you didn't know her. You've only just arrived. Not what they would call a great start to your arrival here."

"Oh, I don't see it that way. People come and go. You carry on."

"Yes. I suppose that's a truism. My name is Ryan, Ryan East."

"Quinlan Taylor. You bake bread, so that name's appropriate. Rye and Yeast, Ryan East."

"Ah, yes. I hadn't thought of it! East or yeast, though I dabble in sourdough. But yes, even that could technically be called yeast. That's funny!"

Quinlan smiled and said, "Looks like we're going to be neighbours. Also, competitors of sorts."

"Oh, do you plan to start a bakery as well? That would become very interesting!"

"Baking, yes, but not bread. At least, not to start. Cupcakes, pastries, that sort of thing."

"Ah, well, that would be complementary to bread, not really a competitor. Welcome to the neighbourhood."

A month later, the interior construction work opposite was completed and the sign went up.

QT's Cupcakes.

Ryan hadn't had much to do with the long legged neighbour and she had been busy supervising the renovation work. The town was keenly aware that the new business would offer something more than the usual breads and buns from Ryan's shop.

The opening day arrived in a flurry of pink. The shelves were lined with pink satin, the decorations consisted of pink tassels, pink glitter along the windowsills and pink balloons swung gently in the breeze.

Ryan's bakery looked decidedly staid, in its oak panelled antiquity. The pinkness lasted the entire week. The cupcakes sold well, and made a small dent in Ryan's sales.

He sat with the books at the end of the first week and mapped out the sales trends. A decided lean downwards, he thought, but it was early days. The Curiosity Bump, he called it, whenever a new product became available it seemed that many tried it out of curiosity. The regular trend would appear. As of now, it seemed, there was nothing to worry about.

The next evening, Ryan entered the pub at his usual time. He took his pint over to his table and found QT sitting there with her glass of beer.

"Ah. Mind if I join you? We haven't had a chance to connect, given we're neighbours."

She waved him to the seat opposite her.

"My first time here. I was wondering if I would know anyone. A couple of people nodded but nobody seemed to want to talk to me."

"I guess they are shy around here. How are you? How did the first week go? I must say all that pink made the shop, um, stand out!"

"They're not used to pink here! Right! I noticed. Everything here is old and antique."

"Like me, and my bakery", said Ryan, lifting his glass to her.

"You know what I mean! I don't mean to be rude. It's just.... Different. That's all."

"Well, did it meet your expectations, the first week?"

"Oh yes. People came out of curiosity you know. I call it the Novelty Curve. People will come to check it out. It's the weeks after the first wave that will tell us more."

Ryan's eyebrows were raised and his lips curled, so he hurriedly picked up his glass and took a long draught.

She watched him, her head cocked.

"Your reaction there. You seemed surprised or amused. Which is it?"

Ryan wiped the table and put his glass down.

"Both, to be clear. I call it the Curiosity Bump, so we're seeing the same thing."

She burst into laughter, a rich peal that showed perfect white teeth and a neck that had faint lines of age.

"Imagine that! We have two things in common now! We bake and we're aligned on the product introduction cycle. Thirty five years managing products and there I am, thousands of miles away from New York, and who should I be competing with, but another product guy!"

"Well, to be clear. I wasn't a product manager. I was an actuary, but I got to weigh in on lots of products and the harebrained ideas of product managers."

"Ah, so I'm harebrained, am I! Wow! That's comforting to know!"

"It's not an insult. A lot of the harebrained ideas were actually quite clever. You have to have ideas, you can't survive without them. But you have to test them. It's the testing and research where people fail. You know, it becomes a pet project of someone high up and then a lot of effort and money is spent on producing it. Without adequate testing."

Quinlan put her hand out.

"Thank you. You are right, though. Truce?"

Ryan took her hand, and said "Truce."

She sat back and smiled at him.

"This is my first time in here. Do you come in here often?"

"A couple of times a week, over the weekends. I'm still the new guy here. They call me Mr. East, not Ryan. See, I've only been here for five years. I moved here from the city after retirement."

"Not like that poor old lady who collapsed in your store."

"Yes. A lifelong resident, an institution. Rumour has it she was born here, before the town was built."

Ryan expected her to laugh, but she didn't, which confused him a little.

"It's odd, to me, to see folks living in the same place all their lives. I've never set roots anywhere. And now here I am, so far removed from all the places I lived in in the States."

"So you're American?"

"Born and bred, as we say. Midwest, briefly, before we moved around a bit. Ohio, Kentucky, and then upstate New York. I went to Syracuse for college and got me a job and then more moving, until New York gave me a chance to settle before I retired."

"Oh, I understand that. You settled down to retire and moved to England, bought yourself a cottage and a small business baking. That's settling down."

"You're making fun of me, aren't you?"

"Oh, no, no. I do understand what you meant by settling down to retire. A lot of the folks I used to work with don't understand why I moved here and wake up at some ungodly hour to start working."

"Hmm. Ok. I accept your apology."

"It wasn't an apology. It was an explanation. Those people wanted me to settle down quietly, wake up late, read the news, go for a walk, of course, with my walking stick, write letters to the editor, make tea and talk to a cat."

"Ah, their idea of retirement. They aren't close to retirement so they don't understand. Yep."

"Speaking of retirement, it is past eight, so I'm going to get on home and get to bed. Tomorrow is another day of looking after rye and yeast."

"You're not going to let me forget that silly joke, are you?"
"Never."
"Well, you have that now! You live above the bakery, right? I've seen you at the window, after a hard day baking and selling. Drinking coffee."
"Yes. I've noticed you noticing me drinking coffee."
"Tell me about you. You seem to know about products, but you don't quite sound like it was fully your thing."

Ryan nodded.

"Yeah. You got me. I was an actuary, as I said, who made a bit of money talking about risk. Apparently, all good product folk want someone to chat with about the risks of new stuff they desperately, eagerly want to produce. And sell for large sums of money to large groups of the unsuspecting populace."

It was Quinlan's turn to nod in agreement.

"Where were you when I needed someone like that? What about kids, family? Nobody to come visit?"

She saw the expression on his face and quickly put her hand on his.

"No. Please. Don't answer that. It was rude of me to pry. I shouldn't have."

"Ah. It's ok. It's not a secret. I never got married and never had kids. I was almost engaged once, then found out that she didn't actually like me. So she said no, and left."

"Oh. A risk you didn't see coming when you calculated it was ok to propose!"

"Yes. My biggest failure."

"Well, let me tell you about me."

"You don't have to, Quinlan."

"Please call me QT. Everyone does. Quinlan is such a stupid name and, on top of that, it's a mouthful."

"I uh it feels weird calling you QT. What if someone was to hear me calling you a cutie? It would be so embarrassing!"

"For you! Not for me. Everyone has always called me QT. It did raise a few eyebrows a couple of times, but never more than a few hundred times. I don't hate my parents, though, if I remember my mom, she was ditsy, quite ditsy. I think she thought it was..."

"Cute?"

Ryan's grin was met with a peal of laughter from Quinlan.

"Anyway, I have, also, never been married. I think, I intimidate the guys. I'm too tall."

"Nonsense! What does 'too tall' mean?"

"Well, that's what one of them said."

"Yes. I get that. I had a girl call me too witty."

"Losers! Those people don't know what they've lost."

"A lot of people would say, that you and I are losers, actually!"

Quinlan grinned and said, "Well, loser #2, shall we head out?

They walked out, chatting, the five minutes back to their houses. Goodnights exchanged, Ryan went in, changed and got into bed.

The next morning, he woke late because his alarm hadn't gone off. He realized that the shop was closed and he didn't have to bake anything. He looked at the watch and it was nearly six. He lay back, staring at the ceiling, his brain full of the conversation with Quinlan last evening.

When the need for coffee finally drove him down to the kitchen, an hour later, he busied himself toasting bread, making coffee and sitting down in the easy chair in the little garden at the front of the house.

He could see that QT's Cupcakes was open for business. He drank his coffee, watching the people who entered and tried to gauge what they were carrying as they left. He noted that some didn't seem to be carrying anything at all.

He heaved himself out of his chair and walked across into the shop.

QT was there, her hair in a bun under a net, sporting a red, pink and white checked apron that came up to her neck.

She was attending to a young family, with two children, aged somewhere between eight and ten. The boy sounded plaintive and sulky, his younger sister was moving from side to side, possibly excited by what she was about to get as a treat.

QT looked up, smiled and nodded at Ryan. She busied herself packing up the pastries for the family and processing their payment.

As they left, she said, "And what can I get you, Mr. East?"

"Oooh, I thought we were friends! Mr. East!"

"Ryan. Can I get you something? Try something! I know, try this lemon tart."

"I suppose, I will. How much is that?"

"Hardly any calories, but yeah, sugar, is another story."

"Price, QT, price! I can't take advantage of you by getting freebies! Next thing I know, you'll be over at the bakery wanting free stuff!"

She gave him a withering look, and a paper napkin with the tart on it.

He took it, grimaced and took a tentative nibble.

"Oh go on! Eat it!"

"Oh all right then!"

He chewed meditatively, took another bite, his mouth moving, his eyes and nose showing how he was lost in evaluating the tart, in a near perfect imitation of a wine connoisseur.

She watched him, shaking her head, trying to stifle her laughter, as he inspected the now empty paper napkin, took a last sniff at it.

"I definitely detected overtones of lemon, with a flour base. The flour is probably from the grocery store region. It has a distinct finish of fruit, with hints of sugar from the box."

"You're an idiot!" she said, as she burst out laughing.

"How about some coffee with it?"

She stuck her lower lip out and said, "I don't do coffee. I don't have space and anyway, as an American, I'm told we folks don't know coffee."

"I agree. You people dole out that watered down rubbish and truly don't understand coffee. So would you like some? I have this big coffee maker and my customers can get a coffee with their boule."

"Well, la de dah! Get me a cup, then, and be quick about it!"

He nodded and left with raised eyebrows.

"Watch out for QT, there, she's in a mood and she hasn't had her coffee yet", he said to the couple who stood aside to let him out.

The lady giggled and said "Thanks!"

And so the tradition was started. A daily cup of coffee was delivered across the street. Some days when he was busier than normal, Ryan would ask one the regulars if they would mind stepping across the street to deliver the cup of coffee.

The coffee was usually repaid by a cupcake that would head across the street the other way. The crossing of customers became a standard feature. Some of the more romantic and playful regulars on both sides, offered to do the cross street deliveries, even when Ryan was free, laughing as they did.

Three months passed as the town got into the act. Gossip and rumours were rife, but nobody had ever seen Ryan and Quinlan together. They met, when they did, at the pub. Over beer, the conversation flowed smoothly.

Ryan's bakery was closed on Mondays, Quinlan's cupcake shop was closed on Thursdays. This meant the pub meetings didn't happen as often as Ryan would have liked. He found himself missing sitting across from her on Sunday evenings, which had been his usual day at the pub.

Then one day, he spotted a new sign going up across the street.

'Please note our new hours! Closed on Mondays!'

He chuckled to himself and the morning went with customers standing in his shop, chatting with an unusually talkative Ryan. Around eleven, he told the customers, to pick whatever they wanted and leave the money behind, because he had to attend something briefly.

The people all came to the door to see him walk across to QT's with a cheese and spinach loaf in one hand and a coffee in the other. He was gone for a full ten minutes.

They stepped out to see a cheer go up from the people waiting outside. The two bakers stepped out into the middle of the street with smiles on their faces. They waved at the people cheering, before heading back to their respective shops.

Sunday evenings at the pub became a regular feature. It was in one of those evenings at the pub, that Ryan said, "You know, I'm going to offer a suggestion. Why don't we..."

"Cross sell products. Yep. Why not indeed."

"I forgot for a minute there that you were one of those hare... I mean, product people. Yeah. Why don't we? Offer bundles. Two coffees with a six-pack of QT cupcakes. And I can offer, now what can I offer, let me think. Buy a coffee and a boule and you get two cupcakes from QT."

They spent the next month finetuning the bundled offerings.

It became apparent, rather quickly, that this was not working for people. It seemed that, Ryan's steady and oldfashioned manner towards customers worked for a certain category of consumers. Others, however, liked the bright ambience of QT's Cupcakes. QT herself was always there, adding to the brightness of the products on display.

There was a natural divide and a solution was needed.

"We need to work this out. Clearly, we have an issue with the user engagement."

"Yes. And never the twain shall meet. Yes. So what do we do?"

"Um... yeah", Ryan took a sip of his beer, put down the glass and looked down at the table.

He cleared this throat.

"Out with it, Ryan! Are you going to suggest what I think you're going to suggest?"

"Well, you know, when we had these kinds of issues, we usually ended up in a holiday resort somewhere, by the beach or a golf course. You know, play during the day and plan during the night over endless supplies of alcohol written off in the books as planning expenses."

"Oh, my gawd! You, nasty old man! What an absolutely wonderful idea!"

"What?"

"It's perfect! That's exactly what we should do! It's what we would have done back at work. Why not?"

"You mean, you'll come?"

"Of course! What makes you think I wouldn't?"

"Well, you know, I ah..."

"Drink up and run home. You have to plan this thing!"

The gossip in town rose a few notches as dual signs went up on the street.

"Out on holiday! Be back in three days!"

The train deposited them in a little station with a single platform. They wheeled their bags down to the inn. They were met by a big, jovial lady.

"Good morning! Do you have a reservation?"

Ryan cleared his throat and spoke.

"Yes. There are two actually. One for Ms. Taylor and one for Mr. East."

"Two rooms? You booked two rooms? My god, you really thought this risk through, didn't you?"

Quinlan stood there, with her hands clapped to her head, her mouth aghast. Ryan looked away, not able to meet her eye.

The lady behind the waited, watching the two, trying to contain her laughter.

Quinlan spoke.

"Make that one room. Mr. East has made a mistake. Sorry about that!"

"Mr. East?" said the inn lady.

"Ah. Yes. Ms. Taylor is right. A single room, please."

"And if it has a single bed, that will be even better", said Quinlan.

Ryan felt an arm sliding through his, as the lady clicked through, making sure, the deposit was refunded. Then she handed over a key.

"Your room is up the stairs, second door on the right. I've given you a sea facing room. The sunrise here is spectacular. You should definitely wake up to see it."

Ryan muttered something under his breath. Quinlan thanked the lady and they headed up the stairs.

"I know what you said. You think I didn't hear, but I did! And you're right this time, Loser #2! You will be awake for the sunrise."

"It's a risk I will have to accept, then. Nothing I can do to mitigate it."

"Damn right! You just have to accept this risk!"

Mother's Love

"Ma, where are my socks?"

Julia Griffiths, aka Jules, walked over from the kitchen to the base of the stairs.

"Don't yell! They are always in the same place. The same drawer where they always are""

"Found them!"

Jules stood for a minute, looking up the staircase that led straight up to the bedrooms. She could see the door to Mikey's bedroom was open. She could hear him humming. His feet thumped as they always did on the hardwood floor. She wished he wouldn't stamp so. And why did he have to rush at the last minute. Would it hurt him to wake up twenty minutes earlier?

She heard the slam of the drawer and went back to the kitchen. She poured out her coffee. The toaster went pop and she took a small plate out of the cupboard, took the toast out and started buttering.

Michael Griffiths, aka Mikey, came out of the bedroom.

"Ma, is breakfast ready?"

He didn't wait for a response and came bounding down the stairs in his socks.

Five stairs from the top, his sock clad foot slipped and he fell. In a last ditch effort to save himself, he tried to grip the rail. It didn't help. He fell backwards and his head hit the second riser from the bottom.

"Uh", escaped his mouth, as he finished at the bottom of the stairs. His body twitched, his eyes stared at the ceiling above him. A small pool of blood appeared below his head. His body became still. His eyes wide open, Mikey lay there; the blood seeping slowly across the floor.

"Are you ok, Mikey?" called out Jules.

Mikey didn't answer.

Jules came out of the kitchen and surveyed the scene. She bent over and checked his pulse. With a satisfied grunt, she stepped back and went into the kitchen. She opened the cupboard under the sink and removed an aerosol spray can. She pulled a rag out of the pocket of the floral apron she wore and stepped over Mikey's inert body to the third step up the stairs. She sprayed and scrubbed the stairs above that and down to the sixth, removing all of the wax.

She worked diligently, but quickly, removing all traces of wax. She worked her way up and down the stairs, making sure that no single step stood out as different in cleanliness, color or texture. She took care.

She walked into Mikey's room and up to his drawer. She opened the sock drawer and took out a fresh pair of socks.

Back at the bottom of the stairs, Mikey's lifeless body lay in that stillness that betrays death.

Jules came down and took off the socks Mikey had on his feet. She set them aside and put the new ones on, gently, taking care to see the body was not disturbed. The discarded socks she put into the garbage bin. She them emptied the onion peels, potato skins and eggs shells she had collected on top of the socks. She sliced the edges off slices of bread and dumped those as well, making sure to camouflage the discarded socks.

She picked up the telephone and dialled 911. Her voice was urgent and she sobbed as she spoke of her son having met with an accident at home.

She received assurances that an ambulance would be there soon.

She set the phone down and walked over to where Mikey lay in a larger pool of blood.

"You really should have left home at 18 like other kids, Mikey. For twenty years, you've asked me where your socks are. I'm tired of telling you where your socks are, every damn day."

Jules straightened up, checked her face in the mirror. From the pocket of her jeans, she withdrew a small bottle of glycerine.

The sirens stopped outside the house and there came a knocking on the door. The paramedics took charge of checking Mikey. They inspected Mikey, nodded at each other and spoke to the policeman and his companion who had now arrived and were surveying the scene.

"Slipped and hit his head. Not much to be done. Bled to death."

The policeman nodded and walked to the kitchen where his companion was soothing a clearly distraught Jules. The officers was apologetic but efficient.

"I can't believe it! I loved him so much. He never wanted to leave my side! He's almost forty years old, you know, and didn't want to marry and have a wife and kids and leave his mom."

"Yes, ma'am. So, he has nobody else in the family, except you? No wife, girlfriend? Are there any other children or family members you can stay with?"

"No. He and I are, were, the only people left. My husband passed away fifteen years ago. He left me a nice pension so I never had to work. I like staying at home. I like to read. I like books. Mikey was always home, too. He was so dependent on me and now he's gone."

"Did you try to move him, ma'am?"

"No, no! I don't know much about nursing and I've always read that you shouldn't move an accident victim. I read a lot, you know. Mystery novels mostly, but some romance as well as some classics. I find reading very helpful."

"Yes, ma'am. So you were in the kitchen when he fell?"

"Yes, I have to make his breakfast, you know! Poor Mikey. I did hear a thud, but he was always very noisy coming down the stairs, so didn't see that he had fallen. I was busy with that toast, that omelette I was making for him. Oh, what am I to do now?"

A strange snorting, choking sound came from her and she wiped her eyes and buried her face in her hands, shaking uncontrollably.

The paramedics removed Mikey's body, wrapped in a plastic bag. Doors banged shut and the ambulance drove away.

The policemen stayed to ask Jules more questions.

"What about your son, ma'am? What did he do?"

"Mikey worked for an accounting firm. He helped out in the office. He took care of the filing and general office. He was quite good, Mikey was. Steve, his boss, always had nice things to say about him."

"Someone will have to call the office. If you like, Constable Mathews here can make the call for you. We will need the phone number, address and the firm's details."

Jules opened her notebook and gave them the details.

"Thank you ma'am. Now, while Mathews here does the calling, I'd like to go up and see his room, if you don't mind?"

"Oh no, his room is right up the stairs. The door just on the right. He came rushing out, you know, he always did rush so, in the mornings. Always trying not to be late, was Mikey."

She held her hanky up to her face as another sob escaped her.

"Yes, ma'am, I'm just going to head up and check. Please wait with Mathews. Thank you."

The bell rang and Mathews held off Jules and answered the door. He spoke to the lady standing on the step outside. He came back and said, "Your neighbour is here, ma'am, and I think she'd be good to have here. Have someone around, you know."

Jules looked up and nodded.

Madge, the lady next door, fussed in and tried to make tea. Jules brushed her away.

Madge, whose relationship with Jules had never gone beyond a nodding acknowledgement, went ahead and put the kettle on anyway. She poured out four cups of tea. The two policeman accepted with a slight hesitation. Jules kept hers aside and left it untouched. Madge sipped hers as she tried to talk to Jules.

The conversation quickly petered out as the two policemen shut down and prepared to depart.

Madge said, "I have to head back home for a bit. Ted, my husband is due back in an hour and he expects lunch to be ready so he can eat and head back to work without wasting time."

"Oh, Madge. Thanks for coming. I'll be alright. You go ahead, Madge. If I need you, I know to call you. Anyway, you're next door."

Madge heaved a sigh of relief as she stepped out and shut the door behind her. She lost no time in getting dinner ready.

She had much to tell Ted, she thought, over dinner. He never had time to talk over lunch, but after dinner, he was relaxed and would be a keen listener.

"That Jules is wonky. You mark my words, Madge! Something weird there. I can feel it in my bones."

"Yes. More potatoes?"

Ted waved away the extra helping of potatoes and heaved himself to his feet.

Once the policemen and Madge had left, Jules made sure the door and all the curtains were shut. She sat down in her armchair, adjusted the light from the lamp over her shoulder, picked up her book and started to read.

Carpe Diem

Andrew stared at the screen shining brightly into his eyes for another four or five minutes, then gave up. He forced himself away from the computer, and poured himself some orange juice and took it over to the couch. His hand reached for the remote and he slouched there without turning the TV on.

Finally, he put it away, and swung his legs over the side and lay there, staring at the ceiling. The flat white of the ceiling stared back at him, matching his mood. When he turned his head to the right, he could see the riotous painting on the wall. Mad little chips of a million colors when looked at close up, they came alive from where he lay.

Sitting up, he held up his glass of orange juice. He closed one eye and peered at it through the faint blue tinge of the glass. Then he switched eyes. The scene moved as the bits of paint distorted, the hayrick heaved and moved. The flaming reds and oranges of the leaves on the trees set them afire. The young couple leaning against the rick seemed to move. Their bodies pulsated and writhed as the light filtered through the glass. Andrew opened both eyes and put the glass down. The painting waited. He blinked rapidly at it. Once again, the scene came alive. He stopped. He put his hand up at his nose, palm out and looked at it. A shadow fell upon the scene.

Andrew gave up, drained his orange juice, and walked over to the painting and crouched a little to look at the bold but neat signature at the bottom; four letters, two syllables, representing a time when she had painted his life with those fine and delicate little strokes.

"Iris"

Andrew stood there, unable to take his eyes off the riot of colored chips, unwilling to remove from his head the image of the girl who had been the rainbow to his blues for six weeks. A quotation from Virgil popped into Andrew's head.

'Spreading her wings, the goddess, Iris, took off from earth, describing a rainbow arc under the clouds as she flew.'

"Damn Virgil and damn all poetry! I need coffee."

He swung around, picked up his keys and drove down to the coffee shop at the corner of Main St and Elm Avenue.

It wasn't trendy. It did, however, have very quiet music which didn't drown out conversation or thought. The comfortable easy chairs were matched with the tables so a casually placed coffee mug could be reached with ease. The coffee was very good, too, dark and creamy. It reminded Andrew of his travels through Europe. The patrons were either older people, seeking quiet conversation and thoughtful coffee moments, or loners, like Andrew, who sat alone with their work.

Andrew Quinn had spent eight years writing.

Burned out from playing corporate games, Andrew had turned off, tuned out, and then dropped out. He was forty eight years old with a receding forehead, an aquiline nose and curls greying at the edges. This gave him the air of a Roman senator, and not just any senator, but a careworn and grave senator. One could truly have said of him that melancholy had marked him for her own.

His writing matched his looks. Andrew wrote dark novels that told of despair and hopelessness. His writing, as one critic put it, "gives the blues a whole new dimension. Angst, despair and morbidity jostle their way through Mr. Quinn's words on their way into the darkest moments a human being could ever conceive."

"Well, hello! We haven't seen you in a while."

The pretty barista smiled at him.

"What can I get you today?"

"A tall coffee with an espresso shot, please."

He leaned on the counter until she placed his mug in front of him. He paid for it, picked it up and turned around to view the chairs.

In the chair he used for his daily perusal of life outside, sat a pale young man in checked shirt, brown khakis and suede loafers worn with no socks. He had a big flabby leather bag on the floor next to him with his laptop on it. Next to him sat a pretty girl with reddish gold hair that Andrew looked mildly familiar. She wore a white t-shirt with a violent gash of color on the front and a pair of white pedal pushers ending in smooth ankles leading to white sandals.

Andrew stood there, momentarily transfixed.

The girl turned her face to him and said "You're judging which chair to use. You can sit here, next to me, if you like."

Andrew Quinn put his mug down and stretched out in the chair with his head back. The girl next to him turned back to the man in the checked shirt.

"So there I was with my camera clicking away. I must have squeezed off at least a dozen shots with different settings in the next few minutes before the rainbow disappeared. I got some great shots for my portfolio."

"Oh, are you a professional photographer?"

"Yes, landscapes mostly. I love rainbows! When I see a rainbow it almost feels like I'm alive just for that moment."

"Yes, rainbows are nice", said the young man.

The girl continued as if she hadn't heard him.

"There must be some cosmic connection I feel, for my parents named me Itzel, which is Mayan for rainbow. That's why I feel so… alive, so full of this indescribable feeling of joy, whenever I see a rainbow."

Andrew's head snapped back and he struggled to sit up straight in the overstuffed chair.

"Nice. I'm just a techie stuck in a cubicle. I wouldn't know what to do with rainbows. I understand how cameras work, but that's all. I sit around producing software code, and that's pretty much all I do."

"Ah, but you haven't seen my photos, Paul! You will love them. Wouldn't you like to see them?"

"Uh. Yeah. I don't know. I'm sure they are very good."

"You should get away from that techie stuff and live a little. Hey, listen, why not come around and see my pictures? You're not doing anything for the next hour or so, are you? My studio is just around the corner. Come on, it's a bit of time which won't come again. It's like the rainbow. It won't last forever. Come on, Paul!"

"Gee, I don't know."

She turned to Andrew.

"You tell him! You know he should, right?"

Andrew sipped his coffee and looked at her, face bright, a little flushed, it seemed. Itzel, the Rainbow. Iris. Andrew's head swirled with memories of the time when Iris had come into his life.

She'd arrived at the end of a particularly stormy moment in his life. He had been sitting facing the door of the coffee shop, just after breakfast, when she had first walked in.

She was dressed in shades of white, a flared skirt in a colorful floral print, a white blouse with a colorful scarf around the neck. Her slim bare legs, which he noticed with interest, ended at brown leather sandals. Auburn hair cut in steps, curled loosely around a face that sported wide eyes, a nose that was neither short nor long. She had a smile that blazed across to the recipient like a multicolored shaft of light, lighting up the room like a rainbow lighting up the sky.

She picked up her coffee and looked around. Andrew, compelled by some unknown force, picked up his bag from the chair next to him. She smiled as she walked over, put her coffee mug down on the table, and floated into the chair.

"I could have sat in one of the other chairs, you know," she smiled, showing even teeth with two extended canines.

"Sorry, I just didn't want to seem boorish, by blocking off two chairs. You deserve the choice. Everyone deserves a choice."

"Everyone? What about those suffering from depression, who want to commit suicide? Should we let everyone choose everything?"

Andrew picked up his coffee and took a sip. She waited until he had carefully put the mug down.

"OK, so now you've bought time to think, what's your response to my question?" she asked.

She held her mug with both hands and sipped, not taking her eyes off Andrew's face.

"I think, everyone should be allowed to. Why should society care if someone wants to end their burden on them? It's not like society takes care of people. We see homeless people, despairing people, neglected people, sick and old people in pain. Society does nothing about them. Why, then, should it get a say in any decision these people make?"

She put her mug down and leaned forward holding her hand out to him.

"I'm Iris."

"Andrew."

"I expected you to fumble your way through a measured response on the duty of every person to society."

"Yes, you did. Did I pass?"

"You did. Do you come here often?"

"Pretty much most days. I come here to think, away from the confines of the house."

"Let me guess. You're a writer. Everyone in a coffee shop is a writer."

"As a matter of fact..."

She broke in, "Oh dear, Andrew. Andrew Quinn. Wait."

She pulled a book out her bag and showed him the back cover. Andrew Quinn stared back at Andrew Quinn.

"Yes, yes! I confess! I did write that. I admit it, freely. Put it away, please."

"Sign it," she asked as she held out a pen.

Andrew flicked open the book and wrote with his neat handwriting.

"To Iris, may the choice be with you always. Andrew."

He handed it back to her and she grinned at what he had written.

"My first celebrity!" she said as she put the book away.

She looked at him and smiled a smile that seemed to cut through Andrew.

"No, I won't ask you about the book. I read an interview where you said you hated being asked to explain the books, and you expected people to make of them what they will."

"Well, that's great then. I really don't like people asking what I meant when a character said this, that or the other. It's a book, read it, and make your own judgements. We judge paintings of artists long gone. We don't get to ask them to explain themselves, do we? Why should writers be treated any differently from painters?"

"Interesting! I don't mind explaining my paintings to all and sundry. I mean, poor dears, they do want to like them desperately, and they buy them so they can tell their friends what it means. Which is whatever I make up to suit them."

"I find that being dishonest."

"I think it's being kind. What's the harm in bringing some joy to someone's life?"

"I don't see the point of all this looking for joy. The world is quite grey, shades of blue and black mostly. The other colors are just illusions."

"Oh, no! You writers are so busy living in metaphoric garrets that you don't see the world at large for what it is. Look at this coffee shop. It's all browns, and whites. It's dark, quiet, even the baristas are dressed in sombre colors. Maybe that's why you come here? It appeals to your need to suffer. Or is it that pretty thing behind the counter?"

"She is pretty and she doesn't seem to have any tattoos or pieces of metal jewelry attached to her anywhere. And no, I have not checked out what lies beneath. I come here, because the music is very soft, the coffee is very good, and I can see the world go by outside that wide glass wall that separates me from it."

Iris laughed, her head thrown back, a full laugh.

"And that's your idea. Observe but be separated from it. Me, I couldn't do that. I need to be in it. I need to engulf it, have it engulf me. I can't stand away, aloof and disdainful."

"I don't have disdain. I just don't see why I have to be engulfed by it."

"And what do you have against tattoos and piercings?"

"Personal preference? People can do what they want. My opinion on it shouldn't control what they do. And vice versa, before you go there."

"Valid. You're right, Andrew!"

They sat in silence, each appraising the other.

"So you're an artist. A painter. How is the market for art? I must confess, I know nothing about paintings. I know even less about dancing."

"Would you like to see my paintings? Or would that be an imposition?"

He hesitated.

"Oh, come on! Don't say no! Be impulsive! Just give in to your feelings and come with me. It's just around the corner. I'll buy you lunch later to make up for it."

And so, Andrew Quinn climbed into the rainbow and stayed there for six weeks.

For six weeks, he watched her paint, carelessly and quickly laying down tiny slivers of color, turning the white canvas into a stormy, passionate riot of color. He watched her cook, slapping simple but delicious meals together without effort, using strange combinations of meats, fruits and vegetables mixed with assorted spices he had never tasted before. He watched her watching him, laughing at him and his serious expression. He watched her sleep next to him, arms and legs carelessly extended over him. He watched the ceiling as he lay on his back, half her body spread over him, a quotation from Ovid, running through his head.

'Iris entered, and the bright sudden radiance of her robe lit up the hallowed place.'

He had known rainbows as fleeting images, little more than illusions of bent light. Iris was real, and for six weeks, Andrew basked in the radiance. Their time together was, for Andrew, a chaotic and confused jumble of events. His routine of waking, going down to the coffee shop, a quick lunch, an afternoon nap, followed by a few more hours of work before dinner was completely demolished.

She didn't have any friends, it seemed. They never met anyone else, no other couples. There were no double dates. She was fully with him. She never asked about his work, never once asked how his writing was coming along. They spent a lot of time talking, drinking coffee, and making and eating food. They oscillated between his house and her apartment.

It was a Sunday, when he woke up to find her watching him, her face six inches from his.

"Good morning," she said, "It's time."

"Time for what?"

"Time to get going. I have to paint you your piece."

He pushed her away and padded away to the bathroom. When he came back she was dressed and sitting on the side of the bed.

"What's happened to you?" he asked.

"Nothing. Let's go make some coffee first."

He cocked his head at the "first."

She was silent as they prepared breakfast, working in unison in the little kitchen.

"Come into the studio."

He sat in the big wicker chair and watched her paint.

"What exactly are you painting?"

"Something for you to keep forever. A special piece just for you."

"Why?"

"It's something I have to do. You were a sourpuss when we met, a gloomy one at that. You're still too gloomy, though I have seen occasional bursts of what you can be. I want you to have something to remember us by."

"Is this what this is about? Am I your behavioral science project?"

"Shush. I'm working."

He watched in silence. She worked away with not a glance at him.

He looked down at his mug and said, "I need more coffee."

She didn't respond. He walked away into the kitchen, busied himself with coffee and looked out of the window. He sat down at the kitchen table, pulled the paper open and scanned the pages.

"Come and see."

She was standing there. Her face flushed and tired. She followed him into the studio.

He stared at the painting, a million or more colors flashing, glinting, moving, and pulsing before him.

"What does it represent?"

"Us. You mostly."

"Good lord! Me? Why me?"

"Why not?"

"OK! Whatever. What are you going to call it?" he asked.

"Metamorphoses."

The next morning, Andrew left early to visit his publisher. He arrived at the coffee shop just after 11 o'clock. Iris, dressed in a silk blouse that screamed color at the world, at odds with the red jeans and blue and red sneakers with Calista laces, was already seated when he came in. He waved over at her.

"I need some coffee desperately," he said, "Want a refill?"

"No. I'm OK. Thanks."

He narrowed his eyes at her and went over to order a coffee. He took his mug over to the little table next to her chair and sat down with a whoosh in the chair next to it.

"I hate editors. Did I tell you that? I hate editors and I hate editing. It's when I start wondering if writing is worth the effort."

She didn't say anything.

"I haven't seen that blouse before. It's, uh, how do I say it? Bright, you know. You're very bright, ultra bright."

"Yes. I like it. I wear it once in a while. It makes me feel better. I keep it for days I'm sad and yet happy."

"Both?"

"Yes. It is possible, you know. A death, for example, should be a celebration of a life as well as a moment of sadness."

"True. So who died?"

"Not who. What."

"What?"

"Yes. I'm afraid, I have some bad news. I have to go away, it's time."

"Go away? Where? When? How long will you be away?"

"Today. I leave for the airport in half an hour or so. Will you come see me off?"

"Wait! I don't get it. What's going on?"
"Nothing. I have to get away. I have to keep moving."
"Where are you going?"
"I... it's not important. Will you come see me off?"
Andrew leaned forward to look at her.
"If you want me to, I will. Are you sure you want me to?"
"Yes, please. I would like that very much."

The ride to the airport was constrained. Andrew, after a few early attempts at conversation and questions, gave up, and they drove in silence the rest of the way. As he approached the terminal, she spoke again.

"Short term parking, please, Andrew. I want you to see me to the gate."

They walked through the tunnel from the parking lot into the terminal. Andrew had already tried asking about her lack of luggage. She carried no checked in bag not even a carryon, only her purse.

At security, she turned and looked straight into his eyes. She put her arms around his neck and kissed him.

"Goodbye, Andrew. I loved you. Take good care of that painting. I want you to look at it once in a while and remember the days you spent with me. Remember to live."

She turned and walked through the gate and left him standing there. He found his car and drove out of the parking lot.

He got off the first exit and drove down to the coffee shop that stood under the flight path. He took his coffee outside watching the runway.

Out in the distance a big jetliner with colorful butterflies painted all over it turned from the taxiway and onto the runway.

As he watched, it gathered speed as it raced towards him. It grew bigger. The wings flexed as the weight came off the nose wheel and then the awkward beast turned into a beautiful and colorful butterfly.

It roared over his head, and he watched it turn into a speck in the sky, the roar of its engines turning into a muted hum.

Andrew Quinn carefully put his coffee down.

Itzel leaned forward, her eyes wide, her lips slightly open as if in anticipation. Fire seemed to dance in her eyes. Andrew leaned forward and tapped the young man's knee. The software programmer shifted uneasily in his seat.

"You know what I think? I think you should most definitely go. I'll tell you why. It's an experience like no other, like seeing a rainbow and you know, you have to enjoy the rainbow while it lasts, because the rainbow doesn't stay forever. You have to enjoy her while you can."

"See? I told you so!" said Itzel, "Come on, let's go."

Andrew slumped back in his chair and watched the two of them as they made their way out to the door. At the threshold, she turned, one hand on the doorknob. His unwavering gaze held hers.

She smiled, waved and stepped out of his life again.

A Child is Born

The house stood in a large compound. The lower floor had a large room where RamPrasad Chatterjee, held court over his tenants and business associates. As the *jamindar,* landed gentry, BoroBabu, as he was called, owned most of the land in the little town, two hours by train from the bustling metropolis of Calcutta.

India had been independent for less than ten years, and the principles of feudalism had not been touched.

The house sported marble tiles in alternating black and white along the shaded corridor that ran the length of the house, overlooking the courtyard, on both levels. All the other floors were white marble.

The bedrooms were large and dominated by large beds, their four heavily carved posts reaching for the high ceilings, beamed with solid spars of wood. The furniture was heavy polished teak, just starting to show the first few signs of use at the edges. Curtains hung at the doors and windows to each room. At either end of the long corridor, wide marble stairs led down to the lower floor.

The kitchens and bathrooms were across the courtyard, separated by the needs of hygiene and privacy.

BoroBabu had three daughters. Sushmita, 17 and ready for a verbal bout at any time was the tallest of the three. Sanghamitra, the youngest, was never far from her books and she could be found lying in bed, sprawled over a *paashbaalish,* book in hand.

The eldest daughter was Suparna, turning on to 19. Her wedding was an elaborate affair, with showy festivities that had caused a temporary interruption of five days or so in the natural affairs of the household. With the *kakimas* and *kakus* gone, and the plaintive cries of *pishimas* no longer piercing the air, the household went back to the regular routine.

BoroBabu dealt with affairs of the estate, from the room at the east end of the house. The lady of the house, BoroBabu's wife, was quiet and ran the household by the simple expediency of letting it run itself, something it managed to do quite well, without her direct supervision.

Alok, the new son-in-law, was 20. His wife, Suparna, was 18. It was natural, almost expected, that Alok would move into his father-in-law's house. He settled in, a strange, slightly angular man, quiet and shy, speaking only when spoken to and then replying in the shortest of sentences. He treated his father-in-law with a courteous diffidence and his mother-in-law with embarrassed respect.

Alok's arrival had made no difference to the life the three sisters had led before the wedding.

Suparna and Alok had a room of their own. Alok found married life disconcerting. Living in the room with Suparna was awkward. She was less concerned with him than she was with her younger sisters, Sushmita and Sanghamitra. Their first few fumbled attempts in bed resulted in a momentary distraction. Alok was shy and inexperienced and she didn't really think it was important. Life settled down into a steady state laissez faire routine.

The girls were home schooled. As daughters of a *jamindar*, the idea that girls would be educated in the local school with the neighbourhood girls was not something BoroBabu had even considered as a possibility.

Every day at 10 AM, Binoybabu would arrive, his cane bearing his weight and easing the pain in his right knee. His grey hair brushed neatly and his *dhoti* starched stiff and spotless, he would settle down in the chair in the room on the ground floor that served as the classroom. As if by clockwork, he would be served his tea, in a white porcelain cup and saucer with gold trim. It would be accompanied on the tray with a plate of two simple biscuits.

It was accepted that Binoybabu could not possibly start the lessons until his tea had been consumed. He would break the biscuits in two, dip the ends delicately in the tea before putting it to his lips. He would chew briefly and take a gentle sip. This would be followed by the second bit of the first biscuit. The whole ceremony was repeated for the second biscuit.

Finally, the cup and saucer were balanced on his left hand and the rest of the tea drunk with a poised right hand. When he was done, hands appeared to remove the tray.

Binoybabu ran his hands over his mouth and chin, as much to ensure no traces of biscuits remained as to signify satisfaction. The girls came one by one, touched his feet, and received his blessings.

Lessons ran until 1 PM. At this time, the girls were shooed away and Binoybabu settled down to lunch.

This included the washing of hands and inspecting the big round copper plate that contained his meal. This was rice, a green leafy vegetable lightly sautéed, a piece or two of pumpkin coated with chickpea batter and fried, a bowl of lentil or *daal* and fish of two varieties. The first was pan fried in mustard oil and spices without gravy. The second bowl contained two pieces of fish in a light gravy. There was a small pinch of salt and a piece of lemon. Dessert was a date chutney with a poppadum. A tall copper glass of water at his right completed the layout. Binoybabu's lunch was supervised by Maltidi, the doyen of the Chatterjee kitchen.

Once lunch was done, Binoybabu, his hands washed and his mouth flushed, would settle down on the day bed. The post prandial nap was interrupted at 3 PM. Lessons resumed until 5 PM, when Binoybabu was served tea and light refreshments and sent on his way, his daily work of tutoring the girls done.

Alok's arrival did not change the routine. The two younger girls, especially, were not allowed to skip lessons. Suparna, now a married woman, had the privilege of choice. The lessons consisted of history, mathematics and languages. Binoybabu spoke unaccented English and never failed to display his passion for Shakespeare. He usually had a quotation ready for every occasion and the girls would suppress giggles when he let loose.

When he was introduced to Binoybabu, Alok was carrying a copy of Spinoza. Binoybabu fell upon the book, and he quite overwhelmed Alok with a minor dissertation on the teachings contained therein.

As the days went by, it was Alok who would seek out Binoybabu and the two would engage in debates about the great philosophers to the boredom of the Suparna and the wonder of Sanghamitra. All of an impressionable 16, she was awed by the breadth and depth of the knowledge the younger man possessed to challenge the elderly tutor. Parry and thrust, the skirmishes between the two were sometimes fiery, sometimes solemn, never without drama.

Alok, read, what Suparna thought was esoteric stuff. Schopenhauer, Nietzsche were unpronounceable names, but they seemed to entrap Alok. He would pore over them, marking passages, nodding as he read, re read and made notes in his neat handwriting in the margins.

Suparna stopped attending classes and spent her time in her room. Sangha would stay on, sometimes asking questions, sometimes making notes as the two men talked. Sushmita would spend her time doodling, page after page of her notebooks were filled with sketches. Pencil drawings skilfully shaded to highlight the play of light were her chosen medium.

The rains came and went. The booming conches heralding the lighting of the evening lamps came earlier in the day. Darkness, as it did in this part of the world, came early. Doors and windows were shuttered to keep the mosquitoes out and the heat in. Woolen shawls sprouted along the streets. Binoybabu's sandals now encased socked feet.

Sangha, who had absorbed all that the previous two seasons had offered her in the form of the deep conversations between Alok and Binoybabu, decided the time had come.

"Alokda, I wanted to show you something."

"Hmm?" Alok barely looked up from his book.

"This. Would you read it, please, and tell me if I have made mistakes?"

Alok peered at the notebook and took it hesitantly. He flipped open the pages and saw the neat handwriting covering page after page.

"Ok. I will read it. Give me time. I will tell you tomorrow, ok?"

"Ok, thanks, Alokda".

Suparna, lying on the bed, put her book down.

"You don't have to, you know. She's a child."

"All the more reason to make sure she is not disappointed, then," said Alok.

"On your head be it".

Suparna returned to her book and Alok opened the notebook to the first page. He read it through and turned to the next and the next. He went to his desk and sat down with a pen and his own notebook. He worked through the page, making his notes and comments.

After dinner, he read it through again, checking his notes. Finally, with a sigh, he shut the notebooks, turned out the lights and went to sleep.

This was the start of the Alok and Sangha sessions. At first, she would write her essay, based on books she had read and present them to Alok for his reviews. Soon, he started suggesting books to read.

Thrice a week, Alok accompanied his father-in-law on his rounds. The two stores, one for general supplies and the other for farm produce constituted the retail side of BoroBabu's income stream. He also owned acres of land that grew rice and vegetables, the bulk of which were shipped to the nearest town and the rest sold through the store.

He also owned most of the builtup properties around the town and collected a substantial sum as rent. Needless to say, while he was involved enough to make the rounds three days every week, the actual day to day running of the enterprise was left to the two managers that accompanied him on his circuit of inspection.

Subir Das was the younger of the two and he, naturally assumed charge of the rental properties. Munshida had been with

BoroBabu a long time and he ran the farms and the two retail stores.

As the eldest son-in-law, and the only one, with no male heir, it was expected that Alok would inherit the entire operation once the old man had passed on.

Munshida, accordingly, accorded Alok the level of obsequiousness that was just one rung below what he presented to BoroBabu, as befitted their relative ranks.

Subir Das was about ten or twelve years older than Alok. Born of a different generation, he treated BoroBabu with deep respect but without the slightly fawning air that Munshida exhibited. Alok, he treated with caution without disrespect.

Alok found these trips wanting in excitement and mental stimulation. He frequently found himself drifting away in the midst of Munshida's quotes of facts and figures. Quintals, kilos, acres were all the same to him. He pretended to pay attention, and in the early days even asked a question or two.

He found Subir even more boring. The travails of some poor tenant unable to pay the rent and the retribution planned for him, left Alok feeling sorry for the tenant and himself, that he was a party to the entire sordid affair.

He went through the motions, week after week, hoping it would end and wishing he was back amongst his books and his writing.

BoroBabu was aware of his son-in-law's lack of interest.

Unfortunately, he had no choice either. Someone had to run the place after he was gone and it had to be a male and a male in the family. Lacking a male heir himself, his eldest daughter's husband was the only hope he had.

He sometimes thought of confiding his worst fears to Sutapa. His wife, ten years his junior, was a fair lady with delicate features and hands, and a heart that had threatened to give way twice already. The last collapse had caused considerable worry among the household and the best local doctors had put out little hope.

She had pulled through somehow. In his weaker moments with his hookah on his porch, BoroBabu thought bitterly that not only had she failed to present him a son, she was probably going to remain frail, sickly, near death and very much alive, long after he was gone.

Still, he was resolved to make the most of it. Meanwhile, Suparna dreamed, Sushmita sketched and Sangha read and wrote. As the winter turned to spring, the household once again came out of its winter slumber. With daylight staying longer and longer, it seemed the house had become brighter.

Suparna, bored from the period of inactivity, proposed a picnic. To everybody's surprise the patriarch stamped it with his seal of approval and the staff were pressed into action to prepare the meals that would be needed. Much scurrying and chopping and frying and scraping took place. The food was neatly packed, wrapped in sheets for ease of carrying.

The grey Studebaker, the only car in the town, was loaded with provisions. Laughing and chattering, the three girls poured into the car. Saha, the driver stood by the car waiting for BoroBabu. Alok, too, seemed to have shaken off his usual diffident mood.

It was, however, Munshida who walked up.

"BoroBabu has work to look after that cannot wait. Saha, you can drive the young people. Alokbabu, BoroBabu's wealth is in your care."

"Ah. Let's go, Saha. BoroBabu's wealth is all ready to go, all three of them."

This was very flippant of Alok; so much so, that Munshida blinked, swallowed, thought to say something, changed his mind and decided to bow deeply with his hands together in an expression of acquiescence.

With their father unable to accompany them, Sutapa also cried off, citing the need to rest and ensure BoroBabu was looked after in case he needed anything.

The drive took over an hour. From a purely distance perspective it was perhaps not worthy of an hour long drive. However, the car was big, meant for the roads of America and not the semi-dirt tracks outside town and Saha was conscious of the passengers and the wrath of BoroBabu should he in some way injure the passengers or the car.

Poltu, the young man who did the oddjobs, sitting in the front next to Saha, was there for the purpose of setting up the blankets, looking after the food and drink and when the day was done of packing everything up for the return trip.

Large trees lined the banks of the river that was more than a stream and not quite a full blown river. Suparna selected a spot in the shade of one of the trees and directed Poltu in setting up the cushions on the blankets on which the picnickers could rest and enjoy the surroundings.

The spring air was warm enough to feel pleasant, with just a hint of coolness. The sky was cloudless and the sun quickly dissipated the last vestiges of the morning cold.

Alok lay, propped up against a cushion, his head resting on his arm. He watched the brook flow past. Just to the right of him it swirled around a tree branch that must have fallen in months ago. It reminded him of a poem, but he couldn't recall which one.

He could hear and faintly see Suparna and Susmita walking away to the river where it bloated into a tiny lake. They sat down by the edge and Suparna took the fallen branch she had picked up and poked into the water. They giggled and pointed. Something very interesting was occupying their attention.

Alok was woken from his reverie by the rustle of a body next to him. Sangha was lying on her back, head towards him, her legs pointing towards the river. From his slightly raised position, Alok could see down the length of her body.

"Why aren't you going over to see what they're doing?"

"Leave them be. They're enjoying themselves. They get along. They don't need me with them."

"They are your elder sisters", said Alok.

"Sure. But they don't need me hanging around. They never really wanted me around."

Alok switched positions, moving the cushion under his right armpit. This way he could see her face, upside down. She had her mother's delicate features. The nose was sharper than Suparna's. He inspected her hand, resting on her breast, long fingers and smooth skin. Her breast rose and fell as she lay there, lost in thought.

He reached out and took her hand, brushing her breast lightly as he did so. She let him have it limply and without moving. He stroked the fingers and became aware that the other two were approaching. Without haste, he released the hand and turned to see Suparna and Susmita running back, laughing as they did so.

Sangha put her hand back where it was, but did not move. Alok called out to the two.

"You girls need to sit down in the shade. You'll get all hot in the sun."

Suparna threw herself next to him. Susmita flopped next to Sangha.

"We saw a fish in the river!"

"Well, where is it?"

"It swam away. It was a big one."

"Poltu, I need something cool to drink."

Poltu scurried forward and busied himself pouring water for the two girls. They drank thirstily. Alok waved away Poltu's offer of a glass.

Sangha sat up and said, "I want to go home."

The others all broke out at once in protest. Finally, it was agreed that they would leave after lunch was eaten and Saha and Poltu had had their meal as well.

The ride home was a quiet one. Suparna and Susmita dozed. Sangha sat stiffly and watched the road ahead. Alok, his playful mood of the morning now completely evaporated, offered suggestion to Saha on how best to conduct the big car over the tracks.

Saha ignored these directions as expertly as he drove. Arrived home, the girls ran off to change. Alok ascended slowly towards his room. He caught a glimpse of Sangha as she seemed to slow and turn back. It must have been his imagination as she disappeared up the stairs and into her room.

For the next two weeks, Sangha did not appear in Alok's study. He sat up late, long after Suparna had gone to bed. His reading took on a ferocious intensity while his writing wilted.

One of BoroBabu's hobbies was hunting. Every once in a while he would pack up and leave, with a couple of the men, Saha doing the driving. The jeep, a war relic was usually used to tour the farms around the countryside, where roads didn't exist and the jeep was ideally suited for the dirt tracks created by itself.

The guns were packed at the back, wrapped in canvas. There was a shotgun and a rifle accompanied by a Webley Scott revolver. This last was used by the BoroBabu to practice, which he did by shooting at trees and tins placed by one of his men at a suitable distance.

After the new son-in-law had arrived into the household, the first time that BoroBabu went on one of these trips he asked, out of courtesy, whether his new son-in-law would like to accompany him. The new son-in-law, out of courtesy, agreed.

Thus was born an unlikely bond between the two. The intellectual, slightly effete young man and the BoroBabu, who was a man's man, groomed for, and now used to, a leadership role and brought up to take charge of the household with an iron fist would disappear for the two or three days these trips usually lasted.

At first, the father-in-law had to teach the young man the basics of gun usage. He was quickly handed over to one of the gun handlers when he found it taking too much time away from his own enjoyment. Alok, freed from the relationship constraint, found it easier to focus on the lesson. By the time of their third trip together, the two were able to separately enjoy themselves.

Alok, as a result of this, started hanging out with the Bidyut, who was in charge of maintaining the guns. After every hunt, Bidyut would settle down to service the guns, stripping them down, cleaning and oiling. He would then place them in the cupboard set aside for them. His job also included keeping an eye on the ammunition and supplies necessary to keep the guns in working condition.

Alok became a willing and eager assistant. Brushing aside Bidyut's protestations, he sat there in the shed and learned how to break down the guns, clean them and reassemble them. He liked the precision and mechanical way in which Bidyut worked.

Alok also started taking the pistol out on his own. He would go off with Saha, out into the countryside and practise shooting at the mangoes on the tree or tins that Saha would carry for him.

As the heat of the summer rose, it was decided that it was time for the annual family holiday into the cool hills. Preparations were made, trunks filled with the needs of the vacationers, food was packed for the journey north. A skeleton staff would remain to man the house. The rest would accompany the travelers. Someone had to look after the tasks.

The train station was about forty minutes away. As the family, staff and luggage couldn't all fit in the Studebaker, two trips were needed. The family went first. The car then went back for the luggage and servants.

The station wasn't a very large station. Two tracks went through it. A single platform lay between the two tracks. There were few passengers besides the Chatterjee family. Two benches in the middle of the platform afforded the only seating. The station house had a small room from where tickets were sold. The rest of the building contained the signal equipment.

The women folk, Mrs. Chatterjee, Sangha, Sushmita and Suparna sat on the bench, after it had been wiped down. Alok walked up and down leisurely surveying the fields that spread on both sides of the railway station. BoroBabu stood near the ladies.

The train was not due for another hour. The air was still and hot, the heat rose in waves. There was no movement anywhere near the station, until Sangha collapsed against her mother's shoulder.

Her mother shrugged and patted her head, but then Suparna started.

"She's fainted! Oh ma! She's fainted!"

Consternation spread like wildfire in a heat encased forest. Water was applied to Sangha's forehead and to her lips. She was laid down on the bench, moaning piteously. Her mother, never very far from collapse herself, was in a marginally better shape herself.

The servants arrived with the luggage and an urgent message was sent to Saha to wait and not head back to the house. BoroBabu took stock of the situation. He turned to Alok for consultation. Alok looked at the girl lying there on the bench, exhausted from the heat. It was then that he saw a flicker of an expression pass over her face.

Sangha whispered something.

Alok and his mother-in-law came closer to hear what she was saying.

"You guys go ahead. I'll go back and stay indoors at the house. I'll be fine there. I don't think I can manage the twelve hour train journey in this heat."

Her mother was twittering. The others had been shooed away to give the young girl some air. As Mrs. Chatterjee looked up at her husband, Alok saw Sangha's eyes open and look at him.

He straightened up and said, "Why don't I stay back at the house as well? Someone has to, if she can't go."

BoroBabu and his wife had concerns, not least about impinging on the son-in-law's time. They had strong opinions on the propriety of putting out their eldest daughter's husband.

The conversation lasted ten minutes, until finally a compromise was reached. Sangha, her mother and Alok would return to the house, BoroBabu would head up the hills with his two older daughters.

Back at the house, mother and daughter shut themselves up in darkened rooms. Mother fell asleep almost immediately. Alok, took to his room and lay down to read. Tea was skipped and dinner served early. The darkness took the bite out of the heat, but the dry heat of early summer burned through clothes. The rains were not due for another month or so.

The night was quiet. With most of the servants gone, the post dinner bustle was muted. Exhausted from the excitement of the day the household slept.

It was around midnight when she slipped into his room. He was surprised to find that he wasn't surprised. When she left, two hours later, he lay there, mildly exhausted with a wild exhilaration.

Every night for the next week, they slept together. Sangha's mother, her hypochondria working overtime with worry at being alone, with a sick daughter, husband away and a son-in-law to cater to, was in poor shape to pay any attention to anything but the mildest activity. The servants, trained from long years of service ran the household with clockwork efficiency.

It was around 2 PM, that two things happened at the same time.

The sky grew dark and a summer storm whipped through the area, heavy raindrops spattering the roof, hammering the windows that were slammed shut by servants scurrying for shelter. A few hailstones cracked down and the postman arrived with a telegram.

The travelers were returning, early. They would be back in two days, and the car must be at the station.

When they arrived, it was with an air of embarrassment and joy.

Suparna's pregnancy was announced to Mrs. Chatterjee and Alok was told in suitably formal tones that he would be a father and the household was blessed to have him to bring the next generation into the world.

The mood of the house changed. The heat was forgotten in the need to ensure that the soon-to-be mother was looked after. Preparations and plans were started.

Alok looked on in dour mood. The nightly visits from Sangha were now absent from his life. She had taken to writing poetry, instead of the minor dissertations she was used to. Her poetry was dark and angst ridden. She had decided that Suparna was to be avoided. In any case, Suparna was caught up in the preparations, with food being modified for her, her sleeping, resting and walking monitored.

Sushmita was torn between the being a part of the prep and her own world. She found that Sangha, too, was available to spend time with her. They would spend time in their room. Murmured conversation could be heard.

Alok, not really part of the plans being made around him, found himself wandering off with his guns. He was now away almost every other day, whenever he could commandeer the jeep. He'd come back with a sulk, sometimes with a rabbit or a pair of pigeons, tired and demand tea.

Before the rains came, BoroBabu was gone.

He slipped from his big wicker chair as he sat with his after dinner hookah. His body thudded to the floor, his lifeless limbs splayed out. Having proved his prediction that he would predecease his frail and sickly wife, the *jamindar's* heart stopped as he fell.

The funeral arrangements and the mourning occupied the household for the next two weeks. Visitors came from the town and the areas around to pay their respects. The feast to commemorate the 11th day of his passing counted some two or three hundred mourners.

The days following BoroBabu's death were filled with a strange calm. The new widow, now dressed all in white, confined herself to her room. Her fragility and inability to cope with stress now at breaking point, she was barely able to function. Even her eldest daughter's impending childbirth failed to ignite a flicker of interest.

Suparna was moved to a room on the lower floor. Access to servants to support her needs was, thus, easier, faster and more frequent. This left Alok alone in his room upstairs. Sangha had not visited him since the time the family was on holiday, but now with Suparna move to her own room downstairs, she was able to visit more often.

Their father's death and subsequent removal of their mother and elder sister from their midst threw the two younger daughters closer together. Sushmita was no longer painting. Talk of finding her a groom had been put on hold in the aftermath of the death and the impending arrival of the baby. In the evenings, the two would lie in the bedroom, chatting late into the night.

The household as a whole was subdued. The evening calm came early. Dinner was served earlier and the activity level after dinner was shorter and earlier as well. Alok, now the head of the household, preferred it that way. It gave him time to reflect and read in his room. The deference with which people had treated him as son-in-law, now rose to a new level. He found he was able to drive behaviour, change the rules and customs as he wished.

The festive season in town reverberated with music, and the sound of conch shells, the drums, the clanging that denoted the prayers were heard in the household.

BoroBabu's house, used to having its own *pandal* which hosted the goddess and the feasting that accompanied the time, was an oasis of calm amidst the joyous celebrations in the town.

The days were becoming shorter and cooler. The fifth day of the festival was the day, the goddess left and the festival came to an end. Alok, lying in bed, reading late into the night, heard a soft scrape at his door. He put his book down and craned his neck to look at the door. It was being pushed gently. He got up and pulled it open. The girl scurried in and he quickly shut the door. She was standing next to his bed and as he walked over to her, he got a shock. It was Sushmita, not Sangha.

He was just about to say something, when he decided words were unnecessary. He clamped his hand over face and drew her down to the bed. Her whispered explanations meant nothing to him. She had talked to Sangha, she knew all about their relationship. She wanted to explore those passions as well. Tonight was the end of the festival and she expected the goddess would understand.

Alok didn't care about the reason. The madness of the last few weeks had grown deep. He let her go before the first of the household woke up, his sexual appetite satisfied. The first awkward moments with Suparna and the businesslike manner of their relations subsequently had resulted in her pregnancy. It had been duty done. He had done his part and she hers.

This new development felt strange. There was exhilaration. There was guilt. There was power. This power was accentuated during the day by his status as head of the household. Subir and

Munshida had transferred their attentions towards ensuring his orders were carried out.

Subir, with his faint air of insolence, annoyed Alok. With Munshida, who was practiced and experienced in the art of serving his master, he slipped easily into his role as the master. Subir he kept an eye on, by instructing Munshida to take oversight over Subir's activities. Subir wasn't happy about having an intermediary between him and the boss, but knew better than to say so.

All through autumn, Alok kept up his gunplay. With the business of running the various businesses needing little intervention and the house running on rails, he had time to indulge.

The nights were busier than the daytime. With one or the other of the younger daughters of BoroBabu visiting him, Alok's life became one of increased responsibility.

Suparna, isolated on the lower floor, now in the third trimester of her pregnancy, would often take a stroll in the courtyard, in the evening before the sun went down. Wrapped in a shawl to keep the increasingly colder air out, her perambulations were very rarely attended by Alok.

The week before the baby was due, he happened to be with her as she ambled along.

"You are happy?" she said in a strangely low voice.

"Yes. Of course, I'm happy."

"They are young, you know. Their chance of marriage was negligible; you realize? With father gone and mother confined to her room, no suitor would be interested."

"Oh. I'm sure there will be someone."

"And now, with what you have done there is no chance."

"What have I done?"

"I know. And you know what you have done. You think I am silly and foolish. You with your books and your writing, you think I don't have a brain. Who is more foolish? You, who can't see what everyone else can because you read books nobody else understands, or people who live in the real world and see what is happening around them?"

Alok turned on his heel and left abruptly. Up in his room he fulminated. He read, gave up and flung the book across the room. He came out and yelled for some tea. That night he locked his door and slept fitfully. He heard the soft scraping and the pressure but did not respond. Eventually, whoever it was went away.

The next morning, he was up early. Harrying the servants, he collected Saha and drove off with his guns. He was gone the whole day, ravenous and coldly angry. Saha, without a meal all day, put the car away and sat down in the kitchen to tea and a quickly generated meal which he accepted gratefully.

The household quickly adjusted to the new patriarch's odd and inconsistent behaviour. All the carefully structured rituals, routines and methods were thrown away. Suparna watched the disintegration, made sure her space and her needs were catered for as before, and left the others to their own devices.

It was still within the year of mourning. The fact that Suparna's baby was a boy, would normally have given rise to joyous celebration. What it did do was allow aunts and uncles to arrive, the aunts clucking their tongues in exaggerated demonstrations of regret, the uncles shaking their heads and shrugging their shoulder in a manly and philosophical manner.

Suparna, tired and exhausted after the strenuous activity of childbirth, paid little attention to the people around her. Isolated from the bulk of the visitors, she was focused on time to recover and gain her strength. Sangha and Sushmita, as newly minted aunts, oscillated between cooing over the baby and fussing over their elder sister.

Alok, given the task of entertaining the relatives, and other mourners, sat in the chair that once was BoroBabu's, glowering and grim, making the most perfunctory noises as the uncles and aunts streamed by and milled around.

Two days later, the household slipped back into its usual lack of routine. Alok's temper was shorter than anyone remembered. In the privacy of their quarters, the bolder of the servants had begun to comment on the days gone by, when the "real" BoroBabu had ruled firmly but with courtesy and decorum and, most of all, consistency.

Mrs. Chatterjee was now confined completely. She was seen briefly the day the baby was born. Aunts allowed to visit her came out, shaking their head in delicious acceptance of her impending departure.

In the evening, Alok sat in the chair, watching the Sangha and Sushmita walking and talking in the courtyard in front of him. His eyes were drawn to Sangha. Her walk had changed, she seemed to be leaning back a bit. He inspected the two closely. It was true, she was walking oddly. His inspection had been noticed by the two, it seems, for Sushmita, in response to something Sangha said, looked over at him.

Alok heaved himself out of his chair and headed up to his room. He picked up a book and pretended to read. He looked up at the soft knock on his door.

It was Sangha. She stood at the door, one hand on the doorjamb, the other on her hip.

"Well, what are you going to do now?"

"What do you mean?"

"You mean you don't know? I saw you looking. You know. I'm pregnant and you know what that means."

Alok threw his book on the bed and stood up.

"I have to think about what to do next. Tell nobody anything."

"Sushmita knows, Suparna also."

"I..."

"Who knows, Sushmita is carrying your baby as well. She just found out today. She's sure. What will you do now? You will be the son-in-law, the *jamaibabu* who ruined the women of the house."

"Leave now and shut your mouth. I'll think of something."

She gave him a long lingering look, almost insolently, then turned and walked away.

Alok sat there in the gathering gloom. He sat all night, his thoughts clambering over each other in the recesses of his mind. He remembered his childhood.

His father, a civil servant in the service of the British, well read in English, was doomed to a life of servitude to the rulers of the land. Alok had been destined for a career in civil service or law in newly minted free India. His marriage to Suparna was seen as a means to finance his growth. His father and mother had died in a train crash a few months after the wedding.

In the early hours of the day, Alok strode down to the shed where Bidyut kept the guns. He picked out the pistol and loaded it. Six shots it held and it was enough for what he knew he had to do.

It was Sangha he visited first. He touched the temple with the barrel of the gun and pulled the trigger. Sushmita was next door, and she died as she slept too. The noise of the two shots had been muffled by the proximity of the targets, but they had been noticed. Suparna, sleeping fitfully, had struggled up in bed, vaguely unsure of herself. She knew she'd heard something, but wasn't quite sure what it was.

Alok appeared at the door, gun in his hand and she knew. She screamed, a loud piercing shriek cut short by the explosion of the gun in Alok's hand. The household came alive and running feet and shouts could be heard.

The servants stopped as Alok appeared in the courtyard, gun in hand. They watched in horror as he put the barrel of the gun in his mouth and pulled the trigger. They watched his head explode and bits of brain flew across the open space. They watched him fall, with a crash, sideways on his right. They watched the gentle whiff of smoke appear at the barrel of the gun.

Screams rent the air as the other bodies were discovered.

Somewhere amidst the mayhem, a baby's plaintive cry cut through the air.

The only member of the family left alive were Mrs. Chatterjee.

And the baby.

Uncommon Pie

The Uncommon Pie was available only on very rare occasions, thus the name.

A meat pie, with a soft pastry crust and a meat filling, it was the invention of the little bakery in the tiny village of Moreton, called, appropriately, "The Baker." It was said to contain a closely guarded secret blend of lamb and beef, spiced with a special mixture of spices known only to The Baker.

It had first appeared on the shelves about ten years ago. It sold well, until supplies ran out about two or three weeks later. It had made an appearance once again about seven years later.

This was when it gained fame. This was due to it being featured in a renowned newspaper column which was based on the views of a single critic.

The critic was a very popular columnist, and he chanced upon the Uncommon Pie, when he visited the area to find out for himself if the hiking trails were worth their mild fame.

His review of the Uncommon Pie and other goods sold by The Baker spread, as these things do, because the critic in question happened to be one with a reputation, and more importantly, a wide following. An influential circle of friends and acquaintances made sure the news was spread far and wide. It helped that the newspaper had a reputation of its own as a supplier of information for the well heeled and, thus, the legend of the Uncommon Pie spread quickly.

The fact that The Uncommon Pie was only available on rare occasions added to its cachet. Three years had gone by since the review that made it famous, and it had achieved a status closely approaching a legend.

Moreton was considered charming and quiet, and it had a steady footfall of visitors because it served as a popular trailhead for hikers. Apart from hikers, Moreton received casual visitors, driving in from the big city or making a day trip via rail. It had one pub, The Speckled Hen, and "The Baker" was the one and only bakery. There was also a convenience store that sold produce, packaged baked goods in limited quantities and basic meat products. These met the basic, everyday needs of the population of Moreton.

The Baker served, as the name suggested, baked goods not available in the convenience store. There were artisanal bread and fresh buns, some filled with homemade custard, some with homemade fruit jams which usually sold out first. There were also savoury meat pies. Everything was baked fresh every morning and the shop closed by 3pm every day. It was closed on Mondays.

It was very popular, and did good business, its daily supply selling out quickly, because the bread was well loved, the pies and buns considered excellent. There were other reasons, not least of which was proximity to the station, on which ran frequent trains to the big city, about an hour away from the village of Moreton.

The storefront was large, oldfashioned and customers were served by the owner himself, clad in a spotless plaid apron and a spotless white shirt with black sleeve garters. His hair was brushed neatly, and sported a slightly greased look. A handlebar mustache and burly frame completed the picture of a 19th century baker.

UNCOMMON PIE & OTHER STORIES

His name was Miles Overton and he had, or so it was said, once been a banker in London. There was some talk of an 'event' that had caused him to give up his city life and move to become a baker, some fifteen odd years ago.

When asked about the Uncommon Pie and the next scheduled availability, Miles would simply shrug, shake his head and say "I'm very sorry. I don't have any information on that."

He had never been seen to smile. His manner in the store with the customers was always polite, and very attentive, and betrayed no trace of a garrulity.

He had arrived in the village a decade ago, as the new owner of the little cottage. He had made some additions, building out to the back and the side. A shiny modern bakery was installed at the back, hidden from sight by the very traditional front, now functioning as the store.

His weekly social visit to The Speckled Hen was scheduled for Sunday evening. He would permit himself two pints of stout and made no more than polite conversation with anyone who attempted to talk to him.

On Mondays, he was sometimes seen driving out in his van. The village went about its business, not caring where he went.

Fifteen miles away, in the middle of what was open meadow, lay Brooke Farm. Brooke Farm was large, covering about forty acres of rolling parkland.

Brooke Farm had sheep, cows and pigs, and supplied The Bakery with all the meat it needed for its needs. Apart from raw meat, it also supplied sausages and hams. It was the sole supplier of meat to The Bakery.

The butcher was a tall, very thin, very fair man, about the same age as Miles. His name was Bruce Arkwright. He had taken over the farm shortly after Miles had arrived in Moreton. It was said that he, too, had once worked in the city.

Bruce had modernised Brooke Farm by upgrading the fencing, the sheds and the farmhouse. He had installed a modern abattoir. The old one was demolished and the new one had modern lighting, a water supply and refuse collection and treatment plant that seemed futuristic next to the shiny stainless steel machinery. It was kept locked, when not in use, for safety purposes and was set back away from the farm, out of sight from the farmhouse, the livestock and the narrow lane through which one drove to reach the farm.

It was not immediately apparent to anyone how Brooke Farm made money. Yet, it employed five farmhands, who took care of the livestock, the orchard and the small acreage of barley.

Bruce Arkwright was as reticent as Miles Overton. The farm hands were often seen at The Speckled Hen. They had very little to say about Brooke Farm. It was a regular farm, doing nothing extraordinary. Bruce paid them regularly, and they got two days off a week. The money was good and there wasn't much else anyone could get out of them.

On the northern side of the farm ran The Hepford Way. Considered one of the most dangerous trails in the area, it started in Moreton and wound its way up the escarpment, across a small waterfall, and up a steep trail. It was especially difficult near the little whirlpool at the base of the waterfall, where the scramble started. There were persistent rumours that lives had been lost there. Across the whirlpool was the edge of Brooke Farm.

Miles would stay the night, whenever he visited Brooke Farm. Moreton had never seen Miles and Bruce together in the twenty years. The people were aware that they were friends, but beyond the weekly visits, the butcher and the baker never met each other.

It was late morning, when the hiker walked in to The Bakery. He was dressed in hiking gear that was expensive and new. He leaned his walking sticks against the counter and said "Hi".

Miles turned from the shelves of bread he was rearranging.

"Good morning. What can I get you?" he said.

"Um, yeah. Morning. I'm here for the day, going to try out the hikes around here. I was wondering if there was something I could take on my hike. What would you suggest?"

"Well, a lot of people seem to take our sausage rolls. Some also add on the lamb pastry and a bun or two."

"I read about The Uncommon Pie. Seems to be a specialty. Do you have any?"

"I'm afraid not. It is not available at this time."

"Oh, that's a pity. I read so much about it."

He looked up to see Miles looking at him expectantly. A faint glimmer of recognition crossed the hiker's face.

"You seem familiar, somehow. I'm wondering if we've ever met."

"I meet a lot of people here. It's hard to say. Have you been here before?"

"No. I think it was somewhere else. May I know your name? I'm becoming even more certain I've seen you before."

"Everyone here knows me as Miles. Shall I pack a couple of the sausage roll and a lamb pastry? It is getting a tad chilly out there. It is late October, so not surprising."

Miles face showed no trace of anything except courteous attentiveness.

"Miles? Hmm. Have you always had this bakery? I used to work briefly with a Miles in London."

"I can't say you look familiar. I'm sorry."

"I know! Miles Overton was the name. He and I worked at a bank."

"Miles Overton is my name and, yes, I once worked at a bank."

"I knew it! I wonder if you know a Bruce Cartwright."

"Cartwright? Can't say I do. You can just tap your card here, please."

"You left the bank shortly after I joined. I was in Technology. My name is Angus Greenwood. Small world, eh?"

He hesitated. Miles tore off the receipt off the payment handheld and handed it to Angus.

"Pleased to meet you. Thank you for coming in. Do drop by next time you're on a hike on these trails."

"There was some chatter when you left about the reason for your leaving."

"It was a long time ago, when I resigned from my place of employment. I thought banking was the wrong career for me. Baking is more my style. If you'll excuse me, I have another customer to serve."

Angus picked up his package and waited for Miles to finish serving the other customers.

"I was wondering, if you could recommend any trails for me. As a local, you know, you probably have a better idea."

Miles looked at him as he did any customer.

"Are you alone? There's the Hepford Way. It climbs up a bit, but it's quite deserted, so you won't meet anyone there. It can get a little tricky near the waterfall, but, I see you're well kitted out. It is on the north end of the village. It's the only one heading north. All the others go south or west. Make sure you don't take too much time over it, as it gets dark quite suddenly over the trail."

Angus smiled and said, "Thanks. I'll try it. How long does it take?"

"Experienced hikers say the entire loop, there and back, takes upwards of three hours. Thus the need to take some food and drink along the way."

"Three hours. Hmm. That should be fine. Have you done it yourself?"

Miles bowed his head.

"I don't hike difficult trails. Are you hiking alone? No friends to share this with?"

"No", said Angus, "no family to nag me! I'm still pretty sure it was the same bank and the same Miles Overton. Are you sure..."

"Good luck on the trail, Mr. Greenwood. I hope you enjoy yourself. Thank you very much for your custom. Do be careful on the trail. As I said, the light fades fairly quickly in the woods this time of year. Now if you'll excuse me I do have to replace that tray of buns."

Angus gave him a speculative look, picked up his walking sticks and left the store.

There were no other customers. Miles waited a couple of minutes and stepped out of the door to watch Miles walk slowly away towards the trailhead to The Hepford Way. He saw him disappear from sight, then went in. He hung the "Sorry! Sold Out" sign out and headed out the back door his house.

The van appeared out of the garage surprising the few Moreton residents who saw it head out of the village.

Miles drove through the lane to Brooke Farm, his mouth grim. He parked the van and walked around the farmhouse towards the shed. He peered in, spotted Bruce and nodded.

Bruce walked up and said, "Trouble?"

Miles who nodded. Bruce grimaced.

"Ok, let's go into the house, and you can tell me about it."

He called out to the two farm hands in the shed.

"I have to get some stuff done. You guys look after this lot."

Bruce leaned on the kitchen counter, as Miles told him about Angus Greenwood's arrival in Moreton.

"Said he was in Technology. Had just joined around the time. I don't think he knows too much, just a bit of gossip. The problem is, he's still there and in the Tech department. He can be a nuisance."

"Hmm. Nobody else has brought this up, since that idiot three years ago."

"Yes, well. Can we take the chance? He seemed to be quite keen on his little theory. Sounded he'd been digging a bit already."

"No. We cannot take a chance. So, then, you're sure he's on the Hepford?

"Yeah. I watched him start out on the trail from the shop."

"Ok then! I'll meet you there. Let me get the stuff out."

He unlocked a cupboard and took out a large package. He nodded at Miles and they walked away to where Bruce kept his all terrain vehicle.

Miles said, "On the way back, when he's tired, near the whirlpool. Usual place near the upper fence of the farm. I'll go the other way on foot and meet you."

Bruce said, "Let me just check in with the guys and make sure we're good."

Miles got back into the van. He heard the engine of the all terrain vehicle maintain an even unhurried cadence. He drove about two miles away and parked the van in a natural alcove where it was hidden from the lane. He walked through the woods upwards to the whirlpool. Bruce was already there.

The day was losing its light was starting to play tricks as Bruce waited for Angus at the waterfall. He appeared suddenly, jumping down from the rock and almost stumbling into the fence where Bruce was sat on his ATV, smoking.

"Oh, you startled me! Whoosh", he gasped.

"Sorry, people do tend to fall into the fence. Which is why I come around to inspect it for any damage. Are you ok?"

"Yes. Let me catch my breath. How far down is it back to the village/"

Bruce looked up at the sky and shook his head.

"Oh, I'm afraid you're going to be in trouble. We're losing light and it's a tricky one in daylight."

"Oh dear. I loved the views from up there, so got carried away. Spent too much time. What do I do now?"

"One option is I get you to hop on to the back of this and I can drive you down to my farmhouse. From there, I can drive you into the train station."

"What other options are there?"

"Frankly, none. You want to hope over the fence. Here we are, easy does it."

They rode back to the farmhouse. It was quite dark now.

Angus got off and said, "Thanks so much! Civilization! Woof!"

"Welcome to the The Butcher, feeding the neighbourhood with fine meats for fifteen years now."

"I've never been to a butchery before."

"Why don't I give you a tour?"

They walked out towards the slaughterhouse.

"I never introduced myself and here you taking care of me and showing me around. My name is Angus. Angus Greenwood."

"And where are you from, Angus, if I may ask?"

"London. Work for a bank there, technology stuff. Nothing works if I'm not around!"

He chuckled. Bruce's face was expressionless.

"I'm Bruce."

"Bruce? Oh, wait! I know you! You're Bruce Cartwright!"

"Arkwright."

The long blade of the meat carver slashed through the air and Angus Greenwood fell onto the tiled floor of the abattoir which was no stranger to blood.

The farmhands were all at The Speckled Hen, downing pints to celebrate the end of another working day. It was Friday, too, so the quantities of beer and ale consumed grew as the evening wore on.

Bruce worked quickly and efficiently, cutting up the meet in manageable chunks, shrink wrapping, labelling as he went.

It was mid November when the sign went up on The Bakery.

"Season's Greetings! The Uncommon Pie is now available in limited quantities! Get yours now!"

About the Author

Ajesh Sharma, is a Canadian author and playwright. He was born and brought up in India and worked for many years in India, the USA and Canada in the technology industry.

His short stories have appeared in The Telegram Magazine and Unbound eMagazine.

His first book, A Couple of Choices, is a romantic comedy, a play in three acts. A Couple of Choices is available in online stores worldwide in ebook and print format.

He is currently working on a dramatic script, two novels and his memoir.

He uses his blog, sloword.com, to showcase his love for wordplay and humor, his intense dislike for cats and his fanatical adoration of okra.

When not wearing colorful socks or attempting to play guitar, he tries to read, write, learn photography and spend time with one wife, two sons, one daughter-in-law, and two grandkids on the outskirts of Toronto, Canada.

You can find more content and learn more about Ajesh Sharma at https://www.sloword.com/

Also by Ajesh Sharma

A Couple of Choices

Milton Keynes UK
Ingram Content Group UK Ltd.
UKHW031118261124
451585UK00004B/439